When A Mother WEEPS

JEREMIAH 9:17-22

MAVIS P. McCALL

AKUA PRESS, LLC
MARRERO, LOUISIANA
WWW.AKUAPRESS.COM

Published by
Akua Press

When A Mother Weeps
By Mavis P. McCall

Copyright © 2015 by Mavis P. McCall

ISBN: 978-0-9765946-7-3

Printed in the United States of America.

Scripture quotations taken from the New American Standard Bible®, Copyright © 1960, 1962, 1963, 1968, 1971, 1972, 1973, 1975, 1977, 1995 by The Lockman Foundation.
Used by permission. (www.Lockman.org)

Library of Congress Cataloging-In-Publication Data on file

Akua Press
www.akuapress.com
Marrero, Louisiana

DEDICATION

MARGUERITE LAJOY WASHINGTON
1994-2012

THIS BOOK IS DEDICATED to Marguerite Lajoy Washington. She is the modest and caring daughter of Margaret Ferguson Washington and the youngest sister of Kendall James Washington. She had a love for dance, and was accepted as a Junior Saintsation, performing in pre-game and half-time dance routines. She enjoyed working with children, and was considering majoring in elementary education or pediatrics. She graduated from Eleanor McMain Secondary High School in May, 2012. She was accepted into Dillard University and was excited about moving into the dormitory in August, 2012. On October 1, 2012, while visiting her boyfriend, she was the victim of crossfire and was fatally shot.

ACKNOWLEDGEMENTS

My sincere gratitude goes to God for shaping and ordaining my life. I am thankful that He gave me a revelation of Himself and placed me on my path of destiny. Only He could take a situation of pain and tragedy and create an opportunity for change. This work, although fictional is a result of my wilderness experience which taught me to totally depend on Him.

I am eternally grateful for godly parents, the late Willie and Annie M. Price, who have gone on to be with the Lord. I will never forget my father's continued example of humility, servanthood, and compassion. My mother passed on January 14, 2015 and during her illness, she encouraged me to finish this work and prayed that the play would move to a national audience. Her words of encouragement have been a pillar of strength for me.

My sincere gratitude for Cortheal Clark, Chair of the Department of Humanities for Dillard University, who agreed to produce the play *When A Mother Weeps*. I am thankful to the entire staff and students of Dillard University who have committed to support this vision.

I am thankful for my entire family rallying around to help with whatever has been needed. A special thanks for my husband, John, and my three children, Felicia, John Jr. and Najah. Of course, I cannot leave out my son and daughter-in-law, Louis and Lacanjala.

Special thanks to Ellen McKnight and Marilyn-Ashton Brown who rearranged their schedules to assist with critiquing and editing this book, at the last minute. The two of you are an example of selflessness. I'm also thankful to the Circle of Literary Friends who share and support my passion for writing.

Finally, I thank God for giving me my pastors, James and Frances Autry, and my entire Cornerstone Christian Center family for your unfailing love and support.

TABLE OF CONTENTS

INTRODUCTION

ALTHOUGH THIS BOOK is largely fictional, it was inspired by three critical events. As a child, I grew up with sisters, so for as long as I can remember, I wanted to have a son. I remember praying to God and promising Him that if He would bless me with a son, I would dedicate him and raise him to fear God. When God blessed me and gave me a son, I was crushed when he became a teenager and began to stray from the values that he had been taught. Then my life was turned upside down when the enemy tried to kill him when a total stranger shot him 4 times. Two weeks after my son's tragedy, a friend of the family lost her daughter in a drive by shooting where she was not the intended target.

When a Mother Weeps, is a candid look at the conditions of this modern era. The time has come when the enemy has heightened his attack on our children. We believers must understand that because Satan's time is very short, he has brought every piece of arsenal he has at his disposal. The prophet Jeremiah knew their land was desolate and that they were in a war that could literally annihilate them as a people. As a result, he called for the women to weep and mourn over the condition of the city. Jeremiah called for the skillful women to wail and to teach their daughters to wail. Jeremiah 9:21 said that death had come into the homes and had killed their children. My heart mourns because sin has crept in and we are attending more funerals of young people killed in the streets than of older adults. The time has come for the women of God to wail as they did in Jeremiah's day. This is a clarion call for prayer and mourning over what has been lost. We must wail over the senseless blood being poured out in our cities. Wail over the young girls whose innocence has been stolen from them before they had any idea what was happening. Cry loud and spare not. Teach your daughters to mourn, for sin has crept in and consumed the land. This is not a story of doom and gloom. Jeremiah 31:16-17 (AMP) says, "…for your work (my words: rearing of your children, prayer) shall be rewarded, says the LORD; and [your children] shall return from the enemy's land. And there is hope for your future, says the LORD; your *children* shall come back to their own country (my words: place of peace and safety and well being)." Hallelujah!

CHAPTER ONE

THE PROMISE

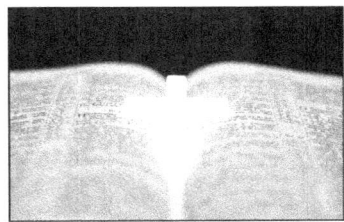

Teddy Bear, Teddy Bear, Turn around
Teddy Bear, Teddy Bear, Touch the ground.
Teddy Bear, Teddy Bear, Touch your shoe.
Teddy Bear, Teddy Bear, That will do.
Teddy Bear, Teddy Bear, Go upstairs.
Teddy Bear, Teddy Bear, Say your prayers.
Teddy Bear, Teddy Bear, Turn out the light.
Teddy Bear, Teddy Bear, Say good night!

It was Friday again, Jackie's favorite day of the week; no homework, a few days off from school, and she could play outside with her friends. It was the night her mom had the ladies over for prayer. Jackie always jumped rope in front of her home and waited for the ladies to arrive. The Thompson's home was known in the community as a place of prayer. When families were in trouble, it was commonplace for people in the community to show up at their door for her parents to pray for them. They had a beautiful three bedroom, two bathroom home with architecture that was unique to older homes in the city of New Orleans, and they always made everyone welcome.

Her mother taught eighth grade at Brighton Middle school and her daddy was a contractor with many projects going on around the city. Her parents were also active in their church. Ms. Olivia was in charge of the Women's Ministry at Greater Mt. Zion Community Church. Her dad, Joseph, was an elder, and she and her older brother, Joshua were involved in the youth and children's ministries.

All the ladies lived in a four block radius and it was customary for them to meet at the corner of Ms. Hattie Johnson's house to make their weekly journey to the Thompson's home. When seven o'clock pm rolled around, Ms. Hattie picked up her purse and closed her front door. As she walked to the corner, all the ladies were there to meet her. Ms. Ida Peterson always walked faster than everyone else and they had to constantly ask her to slow down. As usual, Ms. Diane Sumpter was chatting non-stop. Ms. Hattie had to remind her that there would be no talking once prayer began. Ms. Josie Theodore was the youngest one in the group. She was grateful that God had afforded her the opportunity to be in the presence of such powerful women. They all proceeded to walk around the corner with their purses and Bibles in their hands. As soon as they turned the corner, they saw the police tapes and heard someone screaming. "No! No! Not My Baby! No, God, No!"

They looked down and saw a body on the ground. It was covered up, but blood was everywhere. The ladies proceeded hand-in-hand down the sidewalk. As they got closer, they realized that it was Ms. Janice Theodore who was crying uncontrollably. They all began crying as they were tired of this daily occurrence, some young person in the city dying.

They rushed past the crowd and when they got to the corner of Olivia's street; they saw that Jackie was still outside with her jump rope. It was obvious that they had not heard the gunshots and were clueless that James Theodore was dead. Ms. Hattie told the girls they had to go inside in order to assure their safety.

The ladies rang the door bell. When the door opened, the girls hurried past everyone and went to Jackie's room to play. Shortly thereafter, Stephanie's mother picked her up.

Olivia greeted the ladies with a kiss. When she looked into their eyes, she knew that something was wrong. Ms. Hattie proceeded to tell Joseph and Olivia that young Janice Theodore's son was dead. The couple had a look of complete shock on their faces. Although their neighborhood was usually quiet, they knew that there was no safe place in the city.

Ms. Hattie exclaimed, "God help us! This is too much! Every day, somebody is being murdered. Lord, we have no peace. Babies are dying, God! The killing has got to stop. Lord, what can we do? Oh God, oh God, please show us what to do!"

Ms. Hattie started crying before she began praying. She was crying really loud. It was as though someone in her family had died.

Ms. Hattie said, "The enemy is increasing his attack on the church of the living God. Many believers are fast asleep and not on their watch, while the enemy of our souls is taking territory since the believers are not serious about their faith. He is waging war on the children of the next generation; many of them have fallen into temptation and many have lost their souls. We need to begin to intercede for the children. God is calling us to fast and pray next week. Tonight, we must cover the unborn children in our prayers. He is planning to kill innocent babies before they could enter this world, and there is an all out attack on the minds of young people. That is why the city is unsafe and lawlessness is everywhere."

Then all of a sudden, Ms. Hattie began weeping. Jackie sat in her bedroom and all she could hear was the wailing of the women. Ms. Hattie charged the women to continue to pray and remember that in the end, God was going to be victorious. Everyone began hugging each other and saying their goodbyes.

While her mama kissed the ladies goodnight, Jackie darted past them and went to the kitchen to grab a snack.

"Jackie, don't you dare get into that bed without taking a bath. You have been outside all evening with that jump rope and you are not going to place your dirty body on my sheets."

"Yes ma'am." She got her pajamas and proceeded to the bathroom. As she got out of the shower, she walked to her parents' room, kissed her mama and daddy goodnight, and then she went to her room."

In spite of all the chaos going on around her, Jackie fell fast asleep. As Jackie rested, she felt calmness in her room and her sleep was very peaceful. She saw a bright light and then saw a very tall figure at the foot of her bed. She sat up in fear. Then the angelic being spoke to her and told her not to fear.

It was morning again and she woke to the sound of her alarm clock. The Hallelujah Festival started at ten o'clock am, and she did not want to be late.

This festival was an annual event put on by a group of churches in the city. Many choirs were scheduled to sing. There were many food vendors with the typical New Orleans menu of gumbo, crawfish bread, shrimp fettuccini, boudin balls, etc.

She walked into the kitchen and greeted her mother. She told her mama how she slept so peacefully after the prayer meeting.

Her mother responded, "Really baby, I rested well last night too. I am so grateful that the women of God are serious about praying for the children."

"Mama, I have something to tell you. Please don't laugh at me."

"Honey, I would never laugh," Olivia replied. You can trust me on that."

Jackie started explaining, "I went to sleep and I had a dream where an angel was talking to me."

"Oh, Jackie, that is awesome. I have always prayed that you and your brother would experience God at a young age."

Just as she proceeded to explain her dream to her mother, her father walked into the room.

Olivia turned to Joseph, "Honey. Jackie wants to tell us about a dream she had last night." Her father looked intently, waiting for Jackie to continue.

Jackie stated, "Well, an angel came to me when I was asleep and told me that I was going to have a son. He told me to name him Jacob. He said that he was going to be used by God but that he would have a time where he would struggle with his faith. The angel said God would be with him and see him through it. I am only ten years old and hearing from God about having a child is very scary to me."

Then her father replied, "Jackie, I know this seems a little intimidating, especially at your age, but God has revealed this to you so we can begin to pray. We will learn all we can about the character of Jacob in the Bible, and then we will begin to pray for your child. After church tomorrow, we will start the study, then we will set aside time every week to pray for little Jacob. Once you understand the story, and we pray, you will feel a little more comfortable and then you will be able to trust God to see you through."

Jackie went to her room to get dressed. She was going to the festival with her mother and her brother. Her father could not go because he was in the middle of a large construction job and had to go to the site to oversee the progress. She had decided to have as much fun as possible today. All her friends would be there and she was determined not to focus on that dream. She loved this festival because it was one of the festivals that her mother found it safe enough to allow her to mosey around the site with her friends without constant supervision. When the festival ended, they drove home. As they pulled into the driveway, her father's car was already there.

When she walked into the door, she greeted her father. "Hello Daddy," as she leaned over to plant a kiss on his forehead.

"How is my princess? Did you have a good time at the Hallelujah Festival?"

"Oh dad, I had the best time ever."

Then he walked to Olivia and gave her a warm embrace.

He said, "Did you overdo it today? I hope you let the other ladies help you. You know how you are. Everybody knows you have a habit of taking over. I just don't want you to wear yourself out. Give someone else a chance to be in charge."

"You're right honey; it just seems that every time I try to divide up the list of things to do, something goes wrong.

Joseph looked at his wife in dismay, "Olivia, you have got to trust God and let the women grow. They will never get there if you are going to always take over. Think about what will happen at the church if, at some point, you are not available!"

"You are right, Joseph. I have got to do better."

The rest of the day was rather quiet. They all sat down and watched a movie. Before they went to bed, their mother made the children get their clothes out for church in the morning.

As Jackie awoke, she heard her mother calling her.

"Jackie, get up, we need to get ready for church." She went to the bathroom to wash up, and then she went to the kitchen to rush through a bowl of cereal.

Jackie hurried to her room to put her clothes on. Although her parents tried to comfort her about the dream, she was still uncomfortable. All she knew was that she would have to trust God for something that she did not understand. She hurried and put on her pretty pink dress and waited for her brother to finish dressing.

6

As usual, Joshua almost made them late. Jackie was convinced he did this on purpose. She knew that if their parents would concede, he would probably stay home. This was typical of many of the thirteen-year-olds in their church, who only came because their parents made them.

As soon as they made it to their seat, the praise team began to sing. Ms. Sandra Roberts led the church into high praise. It was electrifying. Jackie loved to hear them sing. As she closed her eyes, she thought about her dream. She tried hard to put it out of her mind, but could not do so. After the offering, she pulled her little Bible out of her purse and waited to hear the message. As the minister got up to speak, he had them to turn their Bibles to Luke 1:26-30, then the congregation began to read. Jackie was astonished to find that the angel had visited Mary, just as he had visited her. The minister went on to explain that sometimes the promises of God can bring pain. He said that Mary had to work through ridicule, the possibility of Joseph leaving her, and the experience of seeing her son being rejected and murdered. He said that her sacrifice brought hope to the world. As he ended, he admonished the church that when sorrow weighs you down, and dims your hope, don't give up; wait for God to finish working out His plan. Jackie listened carefully and absorbed everything that was said.

Jackie left the church feeling more encouraged. When they got to the car, her parents could not contain their excitement. They knew that God had taken the time to bring comfort to their child and they were grateful.

CHAPTER TWO

Beginning the Study

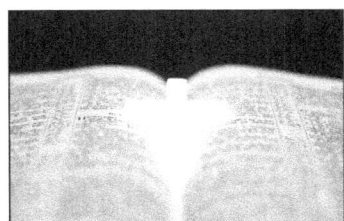

When they got home from church, Jackie changed her clothes and helped her mother set the table for Sunday dinner. Her brother, Joshua, walked in as she and her mother began discussing the sermon.

Joshua began teasing Jackie and calling her Mary. With a hearty laugh, he began to ask his sister, "So sis, do you think you're going to have a virgin birth, too?"

As their father walked in, he replied, "Son, there is nothing funny about this. We must all take this serious. As soon as we finish eating, we are going to study about Jacob, and then we are going to pray."

Then Joshua looked at his father with disappointment. "Don't tell me I have to participate in this study? It has nothing to do with me."

His mother looked at him with a stern face. "Joshua, when we are studying the Word of God, we must all participate. You don't know what God will require of you in order to support your sister."

Jackie and her mother finished up the dishes, while her dad went to his room to get his Bible.

He walked into the kitchen and instructed Jackie and Joshua to get their Bibles.

As they sat down at the table, her heart was pounding. Although fear still gripped her, Jackie knew God would teach her all she needed to know to be a good mother to Jacob.

Joseph began to explain, "Jacob was Isaac's son. He was the youngest twin. His brother's name was Esau. Jacob was a master at manipulation. He and Esau fought before they were born and when Esau come out first, Jacob came out holding on to his brother's heal, fighting to come out first."

Olivia commented, "Jacob was so good at bargaining that he convinced his brother to give up his birthright. He deceived his father and received the blessing that was to go to Esau. This was a Bible custom where the oldest son would receive the father's blessing."

"Wow mama, Jacob seemed like a loser," Jackie replied emphatically.

Then Joseph replied, "Well, Jacob was a smart man; he just used his smarts the wrong way. After deceiving his father and getting his brother's blessing, his father sent him away to Paddam-aram to find a wife. He did not see his brother for over 20 years. In the next town, he ended up getting tricked the same way while trying to marry the woman he loved.

Jackie looked totally confused. "Serves him right, if you ask me! And God wants me to name my son after that guy? I don't understand.

Then Joseph responded, "Don't make any assumptions until we finish the study. Let's get back to the scriptures."

"When it was time for him to return to his home town, he was afraid that his brother would kill him. The thought of meeting with Esau paralyzed Jacob. He had made plans to serve Esau an elaborate meal, but instead of meeting with his brother that night, he had this encounter with *God*, and he was completely unprepared."

Joseph continued, "Jacob was all alone, and terrified of what was to come. Suddenly, he realized that someone else was there with him. This man wrestled with him all night until daybreak. The darkness of night indicated Jacob's condition, bondage, fear and uncertainty; which caused him to feel overwhelmed. As Jacob began to pray, he had no idea that as he cried out to God for strength and deliverance that he would actually end up wrestling with God Himself. It was a long struggle, but when he realized that it was God, he pleaded: '*I will not let you go unless you bless me.*' "

Then Jackie began to laugh as she spoke, "And God didn't strike him dead?"

Her mother replied, "Shhh silly girl and just listen."

As they all began to laugh, Joseph commented, "That's a valid question. Think about it. This was the moment God had been waiting for all along. Up until this point Jacob had to con and steal to get the blessings that he knew in his heart were his. But here he was, face-to-face with the Living God, whom he couldn't con, couldn't trick; yet somehow he knew God had the capacity to bless him beyond everything Jacob had ever sought to have, and love him beyond the repercussions of his actions. He realized he could not get anywhere with God by struggling and resisting. Right then, he understood that the only way that God would respond is if he yielded and just held on to Him. He was aware that he was actually clinging to God and that this is what God wanted from him all along. As he held on tightly, his faith and understanding of God began to grow. In the struggle, God hit Jacob's hip so that it was dislocated."

"Youch!" Joshua exclaimed.

They all broke out into laughter. Trying hard to keep a straight face, his daddy replied, "Son, we have studied this entire story and all you have to say is Youch?"

Joshua shouted, "Yeah man, this is too much! You mean the man had a limp after that? I hope, I will never have that experience."

Olivia explained, "The limp would be a continual reminder of his encounter with God and he never forgot how much he needed God. God gave him a new name to signify that he was a new man. His new name, "Israel" indicated that he had prevailed over his own humanity, and that he succeeded over his toiling with life's challenges and temptations. In this experience, he finally learned that in God's way of doing things, strength comes through weakness."

Jackie finally showed excitement about her dream, "Wow mama, God taught Jacob how important it is to rely on him and not on his own strength."

Jackie's parents could see that she finally understood the importance of Jacob's encounter with God. They knew that this would be an important piece of information as they prayed for her child.

Her father continued. "Jacob's spirit was wrestling against the will of God. Jacob was stubborn and bound by fear, but God found a way to make him submit. You see, before this experience, Jacob did not know that God was with him. He knew that God was with his father, Isaac, but Jacob did not know God until God came to him that night. After this encounter, he knew God. He knew that God was with him. And he knew that he belonged to God. This lesson is very important because it shows us the character of God. God loves us so much that he continues to pursue us. He will chase us until he wins us over. Let us pray: 'Holy Spirit, please help us to pray the will of the Father. Thank you for revealing yourself to Jackie and giving her instructions about Jacob. Please show us how to pray for him. First, God I thank you for forming his innermost parts and making him strong and healthy. Lord, you have named him, and I affirm the words you have spoken over him. I affirm the words of Deuteronomy 5:16 over him that he will have a long life on this earth. I pray that you deliver him from the spirit of pride and rebellion. Have your way in his life and make him the man you created him to be. God, please don't ever leave him or forsake him. When he begins to struggle with You, please visit him and make Yourself real to him like You did Jacob in the Bible. You are his creator, and You know what it will take to get his attention. When he becomes exhausted, he will surrender his will and cling to You. Then the eyes of his understanding will open and he will know the hope of his calling. Help him to hold on to You and never let go. Amen.' "

As the weeks went by, Jackie's parents continued to teach their children the ways of God and the things of God. Jackie was obviously more interested than her brother. They were concerned about Joshua's indifference, but trusted God that all they had poured into him would eventually be fruitful.

Jackie and her mother had many Bible studies alone. Her mother taught her how to pray. She gave her details about the process of developing a healthy prayer life. Jackie learned the pattern of entering into the presence of God. She learned that you cannot approach God with *unrepented* sin in your life. Her mother always said that you had to get *cleaned up* to enter the throne room of God. She told her that sin opens the door to strongholds and gives the enemy access to your life. She learned to always begin her prayer by asking God for forgiveness of sins, known and unknown and to ask the Holy Spirit to remove all hindrances that would block her access to the Father. The next thing her mother would do was to begin giving thanks for God's many blessings. She would then ask the Holy Spirit to open the eyes of her understanding to know the will of the Father. Jackie always watched closely as her mother sang passionately before the Lord. When the singing stopped, her mother would sit quietly before God and wait for the Lord to speak to her. Jackie learned all she needed to know to develop a personal relationship with God. Through the years, she herself began to follow the pattern of entering God's presence. She developed a keen sensitivity of spiritual matters and an ability to commune intimately with the Father.

Four years had gone by. She was in the ninth grade and Joshua was in his senior year at Cajun Pride High School. Joshua was a good student and was graduating with a full scholarship to Holy Trinity University. Her parents had insisted that he apply to a Christian University since they were still concerned about his continual indifference about the things of God. They were ecstatic to learn that he had been granted a full scholarship. They knew that God had blessed him because their pastor had written a great reference letter.

Joshua was happy for the scholarship, but he would have preferred to attend a local college and stay at home. He conceded to accept the offer, since it covered all his expenses.

Joseph and Olivia were trusting God that sending him to a Christian school around youth that had a passion about their faith would move their son. They knew they had done what God had charged them to do as parents, and they trusted God to do the rest.

CHAPTER THREE

It's Tough
Being A Church Girl

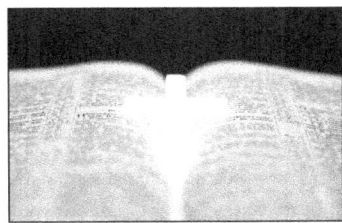

It seemed as if the years had flown by. It was the night of Jackie's high school graduation. Her parents were so proud of her. She was graduating as the valedictorian in a class of 180 students. She had read her speech over and over again making sure everything was just right. Her speech went well and the look on her parents' faces told her how proud they were. Although they were excited, the both of them were struggling with the thought of having an empty nest.

Her parents had finally agreed to let her go out to celebrate with her friends. Lynn had promised her mother that she would take good care of her. Lynn was her best friend. They had been together since middle school. She spent many weekends at their home and was like a second daughter to them.

Lynn approach Jackie's mother and said, "Ms. Olivia, you know how much I love Jackie and you and papa Jo. She and I have been friends since 6th grade and you have been like parents to me. I promise you none of those dirty boys will come near her. I have her back."

With a tone of concession, Olivia replied, "Ok Jackie, you can go, but you have to be home by one o'clock."

Jackie and Lynn strolled out of the gymnasium. Everyone was honking their car horns as they drove off. The plan was that they would get a bite to eat at a local restaurant, and then a friend's parent had reserved a hotel room for an all night party. Jackie had told her friends she could not spend the night, but she would stay until about twelve-thirty, then she would drive home.

They had a lot of fun reminiscing at the restaurant. It looked like almost half the class was there. The manager came out and gave an appetizer to Jackie's table since Lynn had called in advance making a reservation for the valedictorian.

"See that, *church girl*; I am going to make sure that you never forget this night. You have been a good friend. You never stuck your nose in the air at me and I appreciate that. I want you to see how the other half lives. It is not all bad, trust me, it can be a lot of fun."

As they got to the hotel, Jackie could not believe her eyes. This girl's parents had gone all out. They had all the food you could eat and this was the penthouse suite of a large hotel. As they walked in the door, the music was blasting. Since the suite was all windows, you could look at the night lights all across the city, and the Mississippi river was breathtaking.

"Come on in '*church girl.*'" Jackie had gotten used to being called that and she knew that it was really a compliment and was not meant to be offensive.

Lynn brought in alcohol. Jackie did not know that she had it in the car. The look on Jackie's face let her friend know that she was displeased.

"Listen Jackie, we are going to have a good time. We only have one hour. I promise, I am not trying to encourage you to join me, but I am celebrating for the both of us," she sarcastically replied.

"Okay Lynn," said Jackie. "I just want to get home in one piece."

Lynn spoke loudly as if she was intoxicated. "Ok Mr. DJ, the *church girl* is in the house." She pointed to Jackie. "I want everybody to know that this is my best friend, Jackie. She is a good girl and she is not used to being around you nasty boys. So, don't come near her. If you try something, trust me, I will fight you. Now, let's get this party started, let's make some noise!"

Everybody started singing and dancing to the music. Jackie knew the song because they used to always sing it at school. She joined in with the crowd. Next thing she knew, she was crying and laughing at Lynn. She was on top of the table dancing for the entire world to see, and there she was with that bottle of wine in her hand. If the world could not see her, it felt like they could, since the suite was surrounded by windows and you could look across the entire city.

That hour passed so fast, Jackie hated to leave, but she did.

The summer passed equally as fast. She had a part-time job in the mall. She saved her money to buy the things she needed to begin college in the fall. She and Lynn were both accepted to a Sunny Hill College in Baton Rouge and they were going to be roommates.

The time had come for them to leave for school. Jackie's parents agreed to transport both of them to Baton Rouge, since Lynn did not have a way to get there.

They unpacked quickly and giggled the entire evening. They were so excited to be off on their own. Lynn was adamant that she would not let the college environment change her friend. Since her parents had taken care of her for so long, she was going to make sure to take care of Jackie.

"*Church girl*, you have got to be careful around these men on campus. I know the way they are and you don't want to take up with any of them."

Lynn made sure that they took the same courses so she could keep an eye on her friend.

They went to parties on Friday and Saturday nights, but Jackie made sure she got up for church on Sunday morning.

Lynn said, "Come on, *church girl*, God is expecting a lot of you. You cannot allow yourself to be influenced by these heathens."

Little did Lynn know, Jackie was being influenced. Things had changed with Jackie. Her prayer life had changed from spending quality time with the Lord to having these short *good night* prayers.

They got through college just fine. They both graduated with a Bachelor's Degree in Elementary Education.

Somehow, Lynn had loosened her guard and Jackie was now dating this guy named Donald Sawyer.

Lynn thought he was an ok guy, so she left them alone. In years past, she would have never let anyone get that close.

They both got hired at Woodrow Wilson Elementary School as first and second grade teachers. They moved into an apartment together close to the school.

Jackie and Donald continued to date. He spent most Fridays and Saturdays evenings at her and Lynn's apartment, then he would go to church with her on Sunday. Donald was intrigued by Jackie. She was different from most of the girls he had dated. He thought she was the most beautiful woman he had ever seen. She was simple, not all the flashy dressing and makeup. He had gotten tired of fighting for private time with her, so he began being creative and taking her out to eat, to the movies, or to the park, just to be alone. He was also able to convince her to go with him to hear Jazz sometimes on Fridays. He loved her and knew he wanted to marry her; he just had to get up the nerve to propose.

CHAPTER FOUR

'Til Death Do Us Part

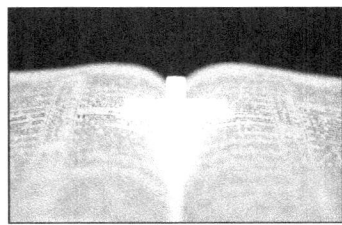

Jackie walked into her parent's home and greeted her mother. "Hello Mama, I had to come by to talk to you. I am so excited; I think that Donald is going to propose to me."

Her mother replied, "What makes you think that?"

Well, he keeps looking at my hand like he is trying to guess my ring size."

Then her mother stated, "Jackie, have you prayed about this? You have only been teaching for a year; you need to make sure this is God's will."

"Well, I cannot say that I really prayed about it, but we love each other and I don't want to be forty-years-old trying to have a child."

Her mother looked puzzled. She could not understand why her daughter was in a rush. "Jackie, don't be ridiculous, you are only twenty-two. You have your whole life ahead of you. You don't want to go through some of the heartaches your father and I went through because we did things our own way without consulting God."

"What Happened?" Jackie replied shockingly.

"Well, we were in love too. We thought love was all you needed to make a marriage work. Boy, were we wrong. We both had baggage. You know your grandfather left your grandmother and she was alone with the sole responsibility of rearing three children. Since your dad was the oldest, he always had to be responsible for taking care of his two sisters. He said that your grandmother depended on him a lot. So when we got married and he began to work, it was like he wanted to buy everything he could think of that he did not get as a child. It did not get out of hand until you and your brother came along, and we could not afford to splurge like that anymore."

"Then I had my own baggage. My father was real strict. We were not allowed to express ourselves. So, when I felt like your father was ignoring how I felt, I would lose it. There we were, two babies and we were fighting all the time. One day, I threw one of my high heel shoes at him. Just before the shoe reached him, your brother came running through the door. The heel just missed hitting him in the eye. It scared the life out of both of us. We realized that we had better get help or things would only get worse. We decided to go to counseling and continued in counseling with the pastor for a long time. Lord knows, neither one of us realized we were walking time bombs. Thank God for deliverance."

Jackie replied emphatically, "Well, that's not going to happen to Donald and me. I think we will be just fine." A quick goodbye kiss on the cheek was a sign that she really did not want or need her mother's opinion.

Olivia thought to herself, *that child is clueless. She completely ignored me and refused to listen to anything I had to say.* She said a quick prayer and asked God to intervene.

Jackie left her parents home and hurried to the store for groceries. Lynn was out of town and she was planning on cooking dinner for Donald. She was so happy to have time alone with him. She thought he was the most handsome man she had ever seen. He had a smooth, dark brown complexion, with high cheek bones, not to mention, a well-formed body.

When she got home, she began preparing the meal. She cooked some crawfish pasta, made a green salad, and baked a cake. She had rented a good movie and bought some scented candles to make the place smell nice.

The doorbell rang and she rushed to greet Donald.

"Hello honey, how was your day?" Donald had brought some sparkling cider and wine glasses for them to drink. He wouldn't dare bring anything stronger and mess up the night by offending her. He wanted to remain in control, but in the back of his mind, he had to be honest with himself that he was ready to take things to the next level. He was happy to be in her life. He could not believe he was in love with a girl like that. He loved her innocence and her beauty was like none other.

Jackie removed the wine bottle and glasses from his hand and gave him a big hug.

She looked at him affectionately, and then replied. "I had a great day today. I could not wait for you to come over. I have prepared crawfish pasta, a salad, and baked a cake."

He laughed, and then said. "You know they say that the way to a man's heart is through his stomach. You must be trying to become Mrs. Jackie Sawyer.

She laughed too, then took his hand and escorted him to the kitchen. They ate and Donald commended her on a great meal. They then went to the living room to watch the movie. It did not take long before things got heated.

Donald looked at her and touched parts of her body that she had never experienced before. She knew she needed to stop him, but somehow the words did not come out. He started kissing her neck and trying to unbutton her blouse. Silently, she asked God to help her, because she knew she was in troubled waters. Suddenly, she grabbed both his hands.

"Donald, I cannot do this. You know I always wanted to be a virgin on my wedding night. I don't want to go any further. I would hate for us to respond to our passions, and then I would be guilt ridden and always remember this night with regret. Maybe we should just elope and drive to Biloxi next weekend for our honeymoon."

Donald replied, "Jackie, I am leaving your house every weekend, full of frustration. I cannot continue this way either. I don't know how much longer I can handle not taking this relationship to another level." He agreed with Jackie, realizing that marriage was their only option. "Okay let's get our license on Wednesday, then go to the Justice of the Peace on Friday evening when you get off from work." Donald went to the bathroom then kissed Jackie goodbye.

She hugged Donald and stated, "Donald, thank you for respecting my wishes and not trying to pressure me to give into you. I really appreciate that."

He replied, "Although I don't like it, I do respect that you want to be married first."

They told each other goodbye as he exited her apartment.

Jackie was so excited. She could not believe she was getting married. She knew that the Holy Spirit had helped her. As she dozed off to sleep, she thanked God for keeping her until she married.

The week went by very fast and Donald and Jackie met at the parish office on Wednesday to apply for the marriage license. The clerk informed them that they could pick up the license on Friday morning.

Both Jackie and Donald took Friday off from work. Donald picked up the license, and bought their wedding bands. Jackie spent the morning finding just the right negligee for her wedding night. She packed quickly and Donald picked her up at two-thirty. They drove to the Justice of the Peace office and the wedding was finalized.

The ride to Biloxi took almost two hours. It was a pretty quiet ride with neither of them saying much. Then her phone rang and it was her mother. She hurried off the phone with her, which made Olivia concerned.

As they drove up to the hotel and got to their room, her phone rang again. It was her father, Joseph.

"Hello daddy," she replied, hoping that the excitement in her voice would keep him from detecting anything wrong.

"Hey Princess, I just realized it's been a long time since we had a daddy-daughter date. What are you doing Saturday?"

"Well? Saturday is not going to work. What about Sunday evening."

"Sunday evening sounds great. How about five o'clock?"

"Okay daddy, see you then."

She turned to her new husband, "Donald that was my dad on the phone and he asked me if I wanted to go out to eat with him on Sunday. I did not have the nerve to tell him that we have eloped and are in Biloxi.

"Jackie, I know this is going to be difficult for you, but we will have to talk to your parents when we get back in town and give them our good news."

"Yeah," she replied, "let's go by the house as soon as we return on Saturday evening. I know they will be disappointed that I did not discuss our plans with them. It is just that it's time that I make my own decisions."

"I am sure they will be upset, but they love you so much, I know everything will be okay. Aftr all, you are a grown woman. It's about time they started treating you like one."

"Donald, my relationship with my parents is very unique. They have always been very involved in my life and I know things have to change now that we are married, but you have to be patient with them because they will need time get adjusted to our being married."

Donald responded, "I understand, Jackie. My relationship with my parents is different. They spent most of their lives focusing on themselves, so I always felt like an afterthought. I have gotten used to not having someone to talk to. I know I will have to get adjusted to the way things are with you and your parents. Don't worry, we will be fine, and we won't have a problem as long as they understand that you are *their* daughter, but you are *my* wife."

"I pray that things go well on Saturday," said Jackie. "It's always been hard for me when I know they are disappointed with something I have done."

Replying emphatically, "Jackie, I have no intention of spending my honeymoon talking about your parents. We need to focus on consummating this marriage. You have had me waiting a long time for this moment and I am not about to get distracted."

Donald had reserved the honeymoon suite. He brought sparkling cider, wine glasses, and scented candles. He wanted to make sure the mood was just right.

He looked at his wife intently, and then he replied, "Mrs. Sawyer, can we begin where we left off on last Friday?"

"Yeah, maybe I can go home with little Jacob already in the oven."

Then Donald said, "I know you are ready to be a mother, but we need to get used to being together as a couple before we add someone else to this family."

Jackie began to laugh, "Well, God will have the final say about whether it is now or later. I will patiently wait for my little blessing to arrive."

Then Donald pulled her close to him and she rested comfortably in his arms. That night was far more than she could have ever imagined. Donald made her feel that time stood still so they could enjoy every minute.

As the morning sun peeked through the curtain window, Jackie's stomach nervously turned. She was not looking forward to facing her parents. As much as she enjoyed her first night as Mrs. Donald Sawyer, she did not have a clue about how to explain this to her parents. Maybe mama was right, she thought to herself, maybe I did move too quickly.

Before her thoughts consumed her, she turned over and saw her husband looking at her intently.

"Good morning Mrs. Sawyer," as he leaned over and planted a gentle kiss on her lips.

"You look worried. Is something wrong?"

She smiled at him with a sheepish grin on her face. "Just thinking about what to tell my parents."

"I have an idea," said Donald. "Just tell them that last night you made me the happiest man on earth," and then he began to laugh.

"Come on Donald, this is not funny."

"Don't worry Jackie. I will be right there with you. There is nothing they can say that you and I can't handle together."

Jackie wanted Donald to get dressed. She asked, "Can we hurry back to New Orleans and prepare to meet with them? I will have to bring some suitcases with us so I can get those things from my bedroom at home."

Jackie sat silently through the long drive back home. Her emotions were beginning to get the best of her. She thought to herself, "Suppose they are really upset. What will I do?"

Her mother was usually right. She hoped that for once that she was wrong and that she and Donald would live happily ever after. She knew that she had not asked God if marrying Donald was in His will, or whether this was the right time, for fear that His answer would not be positive. If things did not work out, she knew her parents would always be there for her, but this marriage thing was all her doing and she would have to do everything in her power to make it work. *It will work. It has to work.*

As they turned onto Beauregard Street, her stomach began to turn even more. Jackie felt like she was about to throw up. As she walked up the driveway, she felt a knot in the pit of her stomach. When they rang the doorbell, she felt like running way. Her mind was racing. *Why had I been so determined to do this my way? I should have prayed about this.*

Her father opened the door and greeted her. He was surprised to see Donald with her.

Donald greeted her father, "Hello Mr. Thompson, Jackie and I were coming over to tell you that we got married yesterday."

Looking at his father-in-law's facial expression, he replied. "I know this is a shock to you all, but we love each other. I assure you that I will do everything in my power to take care of her and see that she is happy."

The room was silent. It was as if you could hear a pin drop.

"I don't know what to say," said Joseph. "This is truly a shock to both of us."

Before her dad could say anything else, Jackie quickly replied. "I don't want you all to worry about me. Donald and I will be fine."

She looked in her mother's eyes and her facial expression told it all.

Olivia commented, "Jackie, I am very disappointed. I looked forward to the joy of planning your wedding with you. I feel I have been deprived of celebrating a major milestone in your life."

"Mama, I don't want you to be upset," said Jackie. "If you want to, we can still have a reception."

Her mother replied, "Your dad and I will discuss it and get back to you. This is definitely a difficult time for us financially. We will have to decide what is possible."

"Okay, we can discuss it at a later time."

Jackie turned to her parents.

"Please don't be upset with Donald." The decision to elope was all mine. I know this is not what you planned for me, but everything will be fine. We all just have to get used to the fact that things have changed. We are not going to stay too long tonight. I will go get a few things and we will come back for the rest of my things tomorrow. Just know that I love you both and hope you can find it in your heart to forgive me."

Her mother stated, "Jackie, we do forgive you. Although we are deeply hurt by your actions, we will need time to process this and to pray and ask God to help us to put this aside. God knows we do not want you to start a marriage in conflict with your parents."

As Olivia shut the door and said her goodbyes, she turned to her husband and saw the look on his face; she knew that Jackie's actions had hurt him to the core.

She hugged Joseph and said, "Joseph, I can see how much this has hurt you."

"Yes Olivia, Jackie is my only daughter. I always wanted her future husband to come to me and ask for her hand in marriage. Now, that opportunity is also gone. What about the joy of giving her away, that is gone as well?"

Olivia responded, "I know, I am hurt too. God will have to help us get over this one."

CHAPTER FIVE

HOPE DEFERRED

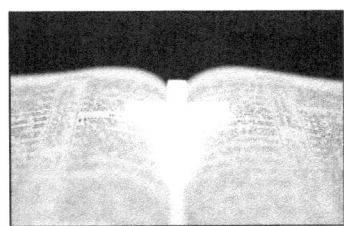

A YEAR HAD PASSED, and married life was blissful. Donald had just gotten a new job and he was excited because he was making a little more money. He was working for the city in the finance department. He loved this job because he was a wiz at crunching numbers. It was Friday morning and he looked forward to their routine Jazz night date.

Donald walked into the bedroom and noticed that his wife looked pale.

"Jackie, what's wrong?" asked Donald. "I have never seen you like this. You can't seem to hold anything down. Do you think you have a virus?"

"No Donald. I think I might be pregnant." His uneasiness was obvious to Jackie.

"Are you sure?"

"Could you run to the store and pick up one of those in-home pregnancy tests?"

"Sure, I'll be right back."

Donald could barely get out the door before Jackie was running back to bathroom for another round of puking her guts out. He thought to himself, I am not ready for this.

"God, I know I have been waiting a long time for this, but it sure doesn't feel so exciting right now."

As Donald returned with the test, he decided not to wake Jackie as she had finally managed to dose off to sleep.

He waited patiently as her eyes popped open.

"How are you feeling, baby?"

"I feel awful. Did you get the test?"

"Yes, let's see what the verdict is."

"Okay. Give me a minute."

As she walked to the bathroom, Donald started to talk. "You know this will change our life completely, if the test is positive."

"It sure will; it's positive," she exclaimed. "We are having a baby."

"Wow. We really need to start saving some money, babies are very expensive. I had no idea this would happen so soon."

"Donald, you don't sound happy about this."

"I'm okay with it; I just worry about us managing everything. I am just starting a new job and I really wanted us to buy a house before a baby came. Besides, this year has been wonderful. I enjoy our Friday night dates when we go to listen to jazz music. I have had all your attention, now I will have to share you with a little person."

"Donald, do you remember when I told you about the dream I had when I was a young child?"

She was disappointed that he was not happy and her facial expression showed it.

"Well, this is God's decision, not ours. We should not be questioning that. God is able to provide for us and help us make the adjustment. We will just need to trust him. Besides, it's not like we got married yesterday, it has been a year since we said *I do*."

"I know you're right. I just wanted to be more prepared. I wanted a little more *Donald* time."

"You seem more concerned about what you want, than what God has decided. If you were not ready to have a baby, you have not been acting like you were not ready. We have enjoyed being with each other and we have not used any form of birth control. What did you think would happen? I am so excited. I have to call mama and daddy."

She runs to the bedroom to get her cell phone, and she dials her parents.

"Hi, daddy."

"Hello, princess."

"Is mama home?"

"Yes, she's right here."

"Please put the phone on speaker. I need to speak to both of you."

Joseph turned to his wife, "Honey, Jackie needs to speak to both of us."

"Hi Jackie, how are you?" her mother asked.

"I am starting to experience some nausea, but I could not wait to call you and tell you that you are going to be grandparents."

"Jackie, that is wonderful! What is your due date? "

"I am not sure. We just took the in-home pregnancy test. I will call the doctor to schedule my first visit."

"Thank you, Lord. We are having a baby. I want to go with you to the doctor, let me know when you schedule the appointment."

"No mama. Donald and I will go and call you as soon as we return from the visit."

Joseph turned to his wife, "Olivia, there you go again. You are always trying to run things. Give those children some space to handle their own affairs."

"Please forgive me, Jackie. The excitement just took over me and I just wasn't thinking clearly."

"No problem mama. We will call you when we get back from the doctor."

"Alright, I can't wait to hear the news."

The next morning Jackie woke up early. She sang as she prepared breakfast for Donald in bed.

"Babe, hurry and eat your meal, then we can get dressed. Our appointment is for nine-thirty."

''Okay, I'll get dressed as soon as I am finished."

Jackie was so excited; Donald tried hard not to let her see that he was dreading the thought of a baby. His mind went back to his childhood and the memories of his mother's struggle to see that there was enough food in the house for him and his brother. He just was not ready to bring a child into this world and struggle like his mom did.

"Donald, why are you taking so long in the bathroom? We have to get going. It is eight-forty-five."

"Honey, I will be right out."

As Donald exited the bathroom, Jackie handed him the car keys and they hurried out to the car. The ride to the office was a quiet one. Neither one dared to tell the other what they were thinking. As they walked into the office, the receptionist greeted them and after a few minutes they were directed to an examination room.

"Hello Mr. and Mrs. Sawyer, said the doctor as he entered the examination room. What brings you to the doctor this morning?"

"Doctor Jenkins, I have a positive pregnancy test." Jackie's face and her voice made it very clear that she could not contain her excitement.

"That is wonderful. I will direct the nurse to assist you in preparing for an examination, then we will try to determine how far along you are."

When the doctor returned and finished the examination, he began discussing the details about what to expect during the pregnancy.

Jackie had so many questions. Everything seemed to make Donald more nervous. He was so preoccupied with his thoughts that he did not realize he had not heard any of the conversation.

Doctor Jenkins directed them to the receptionist to schedule an ultrasound.

As soon as they got in the car, Jackie dialed her mama to tell her what the doctor said.

"Hello mama. I am about six to eight weeks pregnant. So looks like we will have a Christmas baby."

"That is wonderful. This holiday will be extra special."

Four weeks passed and the day had come for the ultrasound. Donald accompanied her to the doctor's office. Jackie waited on the table as the technician entered the room to begin the ultrasound.

Jackie looked on his face as he began moving the instrument across her stomach. He had a look of dismay on his face. He excused himself and left the room to consult the doctor.

Doctor Jenkins entered the room with a look of concern on his face.

Then Jackie asked, "Doctor, is everything okay?

"I am afraid not. I am going to refer your pictures to a specialist for confirmation, but it does not look like the fetus is growing normally. I am so sorry. The receptionist will call to arrange for your appointment with Dr. Chisholm."

Jackie wept uncontrollably. Donald tried to console her, but she could not be consoled. He dialed her parent's number and her mother answered the phone.

"Ms. Olivia, we are at the doctor's office and I am afraid we have some terrible news. The doctor says the fetus is not growing properly. Jackie is crying uncontrollably and I cannot seem to calm her down."

As he passed the phone to Jackie, he could hear Ms. Olivia as she prayed with Jackie. The staff left them alone and it took an hour before he could manage to escort her out of the office.

Two days had passed. Donald could not get Jackie to come around. Her parents had come over the night before and her mother offered to spend the night, but Donald felt that it was his responsibility to take care of his wife, so he declined her invitation.

He helped her get dressed for their appointment with Dr. Chisholm. As they entered the office, the staff immediately escorted them to an examination room.

Donald and Jackie sat silently waiting for the doctor to enter the room. As Doctor Stephanie Chisholm walked, she greeted the couple.

"Hello Mr. and Mrs. Sawyer. I have reviewed the files and Dr. Jenkins was correct. The fetus is growing abnormally and it is my recommendation that you consider terminating the pregnancy."

Jackie raised her voice as she adamantly explained that abortion was not an option. "Creation is God's doing and I am insulted that you would think we would consider making a decision about whether this baby lives or dies."

She immediately thought about her dream. *If God made a promise to me, how is this happening?*

Donald saw that his wife was becoming outraged so he interrupted her. "Dr. Chisholm, thank you for seeing us. My wife and I will discuss this and get back to you."

As they drove home, neither one said a word. When they got home, Donald tried to bring up the issue. "Honey, the doctor is only trying to recommend what is best for everyone. We really need to give some thought to what she has said."

"Donald, I am not about to agree to something that would displease God. If this pregnancy is terminated, it will be God's doing, not mine. He has complete control of this, and I cannot believe you would suggest we do something like that."

"Honey, I know you are a woman of strong faith. I was just trying to end the pain this is causing you."

"It pains me more to think that you would want to make a decision about the life of this baby and not wait on God. He is very capable of handling life or death decisions."

Jackie called her parents. She could not believe that Donald wanted to take the easy way out. Her parents prayed with her, and then she went to bed. The only thing that comforted her was remembering the night God visited her in a dream. She knew that He was not the type of God to renege on a promise. She just needed to wait on Him to deliver what He had spoken to her that night.

She lay across her bed and just began talk to Him. She waited for Him to comfort her as only He could do.

After a week of writhing agony, Donald came home from work and Jackie was in the bathroom grimacing in pain. Donald picked her up from the floor and carried her to the car. As he drove to the hospital, he called her parents to have them meet them at the hospital.

By the time her parents arrived, the physician was examining her. He reported that she had had a miscarriage. The doctor admitted her to the hospital for twenty-four hours of observation.

The next day, as they drove home, Donald tried to make her laugh, but Jackie could not find any reason to laugh. He would not dare admit that he was relieved that it was all over. It was now summertime and his wife would have the time she needed to recover.

He looked at Jackie and he longed to see her smile again. He wanted his old wife back. He wanted to get back to the life they had before this pregnancy. Somehow, he knew that things had changed and there was no going back to what used to be.

CHAPTER SIX

A PROMISE FULFILLED

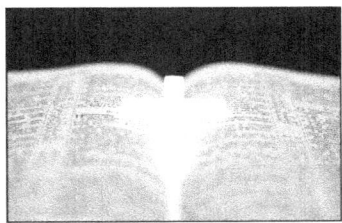

THE TIME HAD FINALLY COME, and their baby was on the way. Two years had passed since they lost their first child. They had purchased a home. Although things were going well, she worried if Donald was really ready for a baby now. He still loved his Jazz nights on Friday. Although she enjoyed being with him, she had grown tired of the nightclub scene with all the married men who had obviously taken off their wedding bands and were flirting with every woman who would give them a little attention. His drinking also bothered her, but she never said anything. She knew that Donald would be disappointed when she told him that she did not want to go with him anymore. Besides, she needed to get back to the active prayer life that she had when she lived at home. It was clear to her now why the Bible cautions believers about being unequally yoked. Although she loved her husband dearly, she knew her focus had changed and her prayer life had been placed on the back burner. She thought back to those days when she could feel God's presence, and how confident she felt waiting for his instructions about life.

It was amazing how much expecting a child had changed her. Her little bundle of joy was almost here. She could see that she was going to struggle with balancing being a wife and a mother.

Jackie moseyed around the house in slow motion. She seemed to move at a snail's pace and it took great time and effort to get things done. The baby's room was all ready. She had packed her hospital bag and she just had a few final things to prepare.

The ladies at church had given her a baby shower the night before and she looked over all the gifts, as she prepared to wash and fold them. She remembered her mother's words when she brought the baby detergent to her.

"Jackie, a baby's skin is so sensitive. Make sure you wash all of his things in this detergent before you put them away."

As she began thinking that this infant would be totally dependent on her and Donald for every need, she began feeling a bit overwhelmed. She shook off this fear and began thanking God that the baby was in His care and she could depend on Him to teach her all she needed to know.

She walked into the spare bedroom and sat on her favorite chair. This chair was carefully chosen because she had every intention for this room to become her sanctuary of prayer. As she started to get up from the chair, she realized that there was water trickling down her legs.

She picked up her phone and pressed one, the speed dial number for Donald.

"Hey babe, what's up?

"Donald, you have to come home. My water just broke."

"Okay, I am on my way. It should only take about ten minutes to get to you. Did you call the doctor yet?"

"I will as soon as I hang up from you."

"Alright, see you soon."

Donald got home quickly and they headed for the hospital. Both of them were silent on the drive to the hospital. When they arrived there they were shocked that her parents had beaten them to the hospital. Donald called his parents but neither answered the phone. He left both of them a message to head to the hospital.

Delivery was uncomplicated and little Jacob came into the world screaming like he had been disturbed. Donald ran down the hall to both sets of grandparents and announced that his son had arrived weighing six pounds, ten ounces, and nineteen inches long.

He ran back to check on Jackie. He kissed his wife again and told her how proud he was of her. He knew she would be a great mother. He wanted to be a good father; he just knew he had no idea how to do that.

The time had come for them to go home. Her mother had offered to spend the week with her while she recuperated, but she knew Donald would not be happy with that, so she declined the offer.

As she lay in her bed, she gazed affectionately at her precious gift. As he nursed, she remembered vividly the night God visited her and told her she would have a son.

"God, you are so amazing. You are faithful in what You promise."

She knew that raising Jacob was not going to be a cake walk. She thought about everything she had learned from studying the life of Jacob in the Bible. She wanted Donald to be a strong father figure for their son, knowing how badly he would need a Godly man around him. She realized that she would have to pray more for Donald. Although he went to church with her sometimes, he definitely did not make God's business a priority.

She got up from the bed and walked to the baby's room to place him in his crib. When she returned to her room, she crawled into the bed and looked over at Donald who was fast asleep. All of a sudden, a feeling of heaviness came over her that she could not describe. Her breathing became labored and she felt a little faint.

She thought to herself. What have I gotten myself into? If I had only listened to my mother and consulted God about my decision to get married. Did I move too quickly? Is Donald really ready?

Jackie remembered the story in the Bible where the Israelites pleaded with God for a king that He had not planned for them to have. God got tired of their pleading and gave them King Saul, but He told them that this would add *leanness to their soul*. Just as they suffered the consequences of wanting their own way, she knew that the road ahead would be plagued by pain and suffering. She knew that this was all her doing and she would have to trust God to see her through it.

God visited her that night in a dream. It was as if she had left her body and was looking down over her room. As her eyes wandered throughout the room, she could see that things were different. Donald was not in the bed, nor was any of his things in the room. Her Bible was positioned on the bed right where he would have been sleeping. She was then whisked outside and as she looked down the street, she saw Jacob standing on the corner talking to two other guys. She could tell that whatever he was doing was not honorable. She tried her best to call his name, but the words would not come out.

When she awoke, she realized that her body had been trembling. She got up from her bed and ran to the spare bedroom to lie quietly before the Lord. She knew from this day forward, she would spend many nights in this room waiting for God's instruction. She closed the door and began to cry.

"God, please forgive me for wanting to do things my own way. I know that I have brought this burden on myself because of my disobedience. I thank you for Donald and Jacob, but I can see now that I do not have the strength to bear what is ahead. I can't see my way out of this. I need strength to endure and strength to fight against the forces that would seek to keep Donald and Jacob bound."

She picked up her phone and dialed her mother.

When the phone rang, Olivia looked at the caller ID and knew that it was her daughter.

Her mother answered, "Hello Jackie is something wrong with Jacob?"

"No, mama, I just need to talk. I am sorry if I woke you up."

"It's okay, baby, I am here for you."

Then she told her mother about the dream and how troubling it was.

Her mother told her to stay strong and continue to pray. She hung up the phone, turned on her favorite song and began to sing.

"I look to You. After all my strength is gone, in You I can be strong."

This song always made her feel better.

Jackie knew that it was time to sit quietly before God and wait for his instruction. She waited, and waited, and waited. Her mother had taught her well. She knew the importance of quietly waiting on the Lord. Then all of a sudden she felt a breeze across her face. She knew the hand of God had touched her. She began to smile. She felt Him and knew that everything would be alright. It felt as if God was rocking her like she was a baby. All she could do was cry because the revelation of His unfailing love made her body shake. She lay quietly until she fell fast asleep.

CHAPTER SEVEN

GOD CAN
CHANGE A HEART

JACKIE KNEW THAT HAVING little Jacob had changed her. He was a toddler now and he was the center of her world. She was not aware that Jacob, not Donald had become her main priority. She had trouble juggling meeting the needs of her child and her husband.

Jacob was now two-years-old. He was into everything. It took all her energy to keep up with him, keep the house, cook, and hold a job.

She did not realize how drastic the change was. Donald had asked her to go with him to listen to jazz for the last two weekends and she had refused to do so. Last Friday ended in a heated argument with Donald storming out of the house. He accused Jackie of being judgmental and ridiculous. She knew she needed to find a way to make it right. She had tried to explain to Donald that she was tired of the club scene. She hated how married men walked in with the obvious signs that they had removed their wedding rings and manipulated young girls into dancing then leaving the club with them. She was so tired of seeing them with their hands all over these girls. Today was Tuesday and she knew that her refusal to go with him again this weekend would lead to another argument. She had an idea that hopefully would make this situation tolerable. She would ask Lynn and her new boyfriend to go with them. She picked up the phone and dialed her number.

"Hello Lynn, I was just wondering if you and Carl would be willing to go with Donald and me to the jazz club this Friday. Donald is upset that I am not interested in going anymore. I thought it would be better if I had someone I knew to go with me. Besides, I am looking forward to meeting Carl. I have heard so much about him."

"Sure we would love to go. I will call Carl and get back with you about a time to meet."

When Donald came home that night, Jackie told him of her plan to go to the club and that Lynn and Carl would come too.

"Jackie, that is so exciting. You know how much I enjoyed our Friday nights together. Having Lynn and Carl with us will make things so much fun."

The week went by fast and Donald and Jackie met Lynn and Carl at the entrance of the jazz club.

The couples greeted one another and then they all went inside to find a good seat.

After they were seated, Donald ordered drinks for everyone; of course, he knew his wife would only drink a diet coke.

Carl began to talk and it was obvious that he was self-indulged.

Lynn had told Jackie a lot about Carl. She knew he was a powerful attorney. Lynn was usually a good judge of character and Jackie was surprised because he was not the typical man that Lynn was attracted to. Jackie could see that he was a charmer and definitely a Ladies Man.

Despite their obvious differences, they were really having a good time.

After Donald and Carl had had a few drinks, Carl began to loosen up and Jackie could see that he was staring at her and it was making her a little uncomfortable.

Then both Lynn and Donald excused themselves to go to the bathroom.

It did not take Carl long before he was trying his charm on Jackie.

"Jackie, I can see that you and Lynn are very different. Your friend is nice, but she is just not the marrying kind. I wonder if Donald realizes how fortunate he is to have you. If I could have found a woman like you, I would have been married a long time ago. If he ever decides to leave you, just give me a call. I promise I will make you the happiest woman in the world."

Jackie knew that Carl had had a little too much to drink, but his behavior was inexcusable.

She was upset that he would say something like that to her.

She did not realize that Lynn had overheard everything Carl had said. She looked at her friend and she could see the fury in her eyes. Jackie was worried because she knew Lynn always had trouble managing her temper.

In a forceful tone, Lynn stated, "Carl, could you step outside? We need to talk!"

Carl turned to Lynn. With an arrogant tone, he replied. "Not now, I am talking to Jackie."

Lynn walked off and stormed out the door.

Knowing her friend was about to loose it, Jackie ran behind her in fear of what she might do next.

"Lynn, please do not do anything you might regret. Carl is not worth it."

"Jackie you know I am not going to sit by and let anyone disrespect me like that. When I am finished with him, he will regret ever crossing me."

Lynn pulled a knife out of her purse and proceeded to slash his two front tires of his S550 Mercedes Benz.

At this point, Jackie was screaming and begging, "Lynn, please stop."

Donald ran outside after hearing the commotion. He grabbed Lynn and held her to keep her from slashing the back tires.

When Carl came out the door, Lynn broke away from Donald's grip and ran towards Carl.

Before Donald could stop her she had lunged toward Carl and began choking him.

As her hand gripped his throat, she began screaming, "Carl you may have been able to get away with things with those bimbos you are used to dealing with, but now you have messed with the wrong woman."

Donald was finally able to pull Lynn off of Carl. As he rubbed his neck, he pulled out his phone and dialed 911.

Donald and Jackie tried to convince Carl to drop everything before the police arrived, but he would not hear of it.

"You don't understand, I have my reputation to uphold. What will people think of me if I let her get away with this? I am an attorney and no one will respect me if I don't pursue this."

When the police showed up, Jackie began to cry as Lynn was placed in the police car.

The officer told them that Lynn was being charged with destruction of property and they could come to the station and bond her out.

Jackie immediately called her parents and her dad met them at the station.

They waited for several hours, and then Lynn was released on her own recognizance. She had a court date in two weeks.

Jackie convinced Lynn to spend the night with she and Donald. She knew Lynn was devastated, although she was trying to appear strong. Lynn agreed and Jackie prepared the bed in her prayer room for her friend. She really wanted to spend time with her friend. She wanted her to understand how much she loved her, and nothing would change that, but somehow, she had to reach her and get her to let go of her past.

"Lynn, I know you had a hard life, but your past does not have to continue to torment you. I can see that when anyone disrespects you or demeans you, it is as if that person is paying for everything everyone has done to you in your lifetime. God wants to give you joy unspeakable. If you could just give Him your hurts, He wants to heal you."

As Lynn looked at her friend, she began to cry. "Jackie, I look at you and I know I can never be you. I have too much baggage."

"I am not asking you to become me. God loves you just as you are. You would not have to change for Him to love you. He just wants you to give Him permission to be *God* to you. I look at you and I see your pain. The things that happen to you do not define who you are. God wants you to give all your hurts to Him. Would you let me pray with you?"

Lynn nodded and Jackie began to pray for her friend.

As Lynn dozed off, she felt a calmness that she had never known. As she dreamed, she recalled her childhood. She remembered it like it was yesterday. She was about three-years-old. Her mom was always drunk, so she never knew a thing. Her step-dad came into her room and got into her bed. She woke up to the feeling of someone's hands under her pajamas. As she opened her eyes, he told her not to say a word. He kept rubbing her until she felt a little sore. This continued for a while, and then he told her he had to teach her how to satisfy a man. He had told her that he would kill her and her brother, if she ever told anyone. It was Ms. Olivia who rescued her. Her mom moved and took them with her, but she struggled with trying to keep food on the table. She remembered how she felt so nasty when he touched her, and then she remembered how it had led her to let guys have their way with her when she was a teenager. He taught her well, she had him to thank for all of this. She realized that she had allowed her circumstances to define her and it felt sickening to her now. She cried, but this time the tears were different. Finally, she knew that her worth was not tied to her experiences; her worth was tied to the only one who could define her and that was *God Himself.*

God made Himself real to Lynn that night. She looked forward to tomorrow. She looked forward to getting to know the *real* Lynn, the Lynn God created.

CHAPTER EIGHT

CAUSE FOR CONCERN

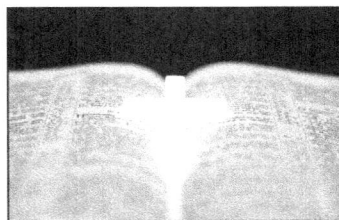

THERE WAS A NEW FAMILY that moved next door when Jacob was five. Jackie, Donald, and Jacob went over and introduced themselves and welcomed them to the neighborhood. They were Gloria and Ronald Franklin. They had a daughter named Lisa that was the same age as Jacob. The children hit it off and both parents were happy that they played so well together.

Jacob and Lisa grew closer as the years went by. Jackie was grateful that Jacob had a playmate in the neighborhood since there were not many younger children near. Jacob was still a handful and some evenings were so hectic, he wore his mother out. It had become a routine that he could go over to Lisa's house after their homework was done. Lisa was always compliant and got finished first. Of course, Jacob goofed off and sometimes he would not get a chance to play with her.

Lisa's dad was especially fond of Jacob and was often able to get him to comply. He had a way with children and Lisa was the product of two parents who knew how to consistently utilize correction, in love.

Donald often had conversations with Ronald about Jacob. He told him that he thought Jackie was too harsh, so that is why he often gave Jacob some slack. Ronald listened, but never commented. However, he had discussed it with Gloria that he thought Donald should be taking a more active role with his son. He just decided to pitch in and help keep the little rascal under control.

It had become routine for Jacob to come over and Ronald would play video games with Jacob and Lisa until it was time for him to go home. Jacob looked forward to those evenings in the Franklin household. Jacob always wanted to win and Ronald and Lisa would let him. Sometimes Lisa would decide to beat him, just to see his response, and it was not good. He would often accuse Lisa of cheating and leave pouting.

When they were in fifth grade, Ronald became ill. Jackie and Donald were there for Gloria throughout his illness. They started having Lisa come over and spend the evenings in their home, while Gloria went to the hospital. Toward the end, Gloria took a leave of absence from her job and spent most of her time at the hospital, while Lisa stayed with Jackie, Donald, and Jacob.

Gloria did her best to prepare her child for the end. They would often have conversations about how much pain Ronald was in. Lisa began to understand that because they loved him, it was best to let him go. Besides, her parents had done a wonderful job of explaining what it was like to die in the Lord.

Jacob, on the other hand, had much more difficulty with Ronald's death. His behavior became more challenging and Jackie felt the void of having Ronald to help her with him. Jackie's father would often come over and get Jacob on Saturdays. He often took him on construction job sites when it was safe to do so. Jacob enjoyed going to work with his grandpa. He thought building things was real cool.

His behavior continued to be challenging and he seemed to have no outlet to deal with the void of loosing Ronald. Jacob continued to try to manipulate everyone to get what he wanted. One weekend when he went to stay with NaNa Olivia and Grandpa Joseph, he brought his box of candy with him, thinking he could get a lot of them sold while there. The candy was a fundraiser for the school. They were chocolate covered almonds and they sold for two dollars each.

Jacob decided he could make a profit if he sold the candies for three dollars, instead of two. His grandpa walked with him around the neighborhood and they sold the entire box.

When he got home on Sunday, he was excited to report to his mother that he and his grandpa had sold the entire box. He had carefully placed the monies in the required envelope. He put the rest of the money in his pants pocket and forgot to take it out. When his mother went to do the laundry, she found the money in his pocket. When she went to question Jacob about it, his eyes got big as if he had seen a ghost.

Jacob tried to quickly think of a good excuse, but nothing came to mind.

"Ah, ah, ah, I don't know."

"Jacob Sawyer, don't you dare lie to me!" Jackie exclaimed. "You had better tell me the truth!"

Donald heard the commotion and walked into the room. "What is going on?" Donald asked.

Jackie replied, "Your son had twenty-four dollars in his pocket with no explanation about where it came from. I am going to call my parents and see if we can figure this out."

"Hello daddy, Jacob came home with twenty-four dollars in his pocket. Could you check with mama and see if either of you have any money missing."

As he came back to the phone he explained to Jackie that no money was missing.

While Jackie was on the phone with her parents, Donald proceeded to attempt to get the truth out of Jacob. He finally told his dad that he had charged three dollars instead of two for the candies.

Donald stated, "Honey, your son has something to tell you. Jacob, please tell your mama the truth."

"Well, Grandpa Joseph took me around the neighborhood to sell the candy for school. I told everyone the candy cost three dollars instead of two."

Jackie exclaimed, "Jacob, you have got to be kidding me! You actually swindled those old people. I cannot believe it. I am so embarrassed. How can I show my face in that community again? Well, I tell you what, you are going right back over there and return every dollar!"

Jacob began to cry. "Mom, please don't make me go back over there! If they find out what I have done, no one will like me."

Donald asked his wife "Is there some other way to resolve this. Why does he have to take it back? I would be glad to take it for him."

By this time, Jackie's voice was trembling. "Jacob has got to learn that he cannot go around swindling people. Donald, there is nothing you can say to convince me otherwise. You should be going with me, but if you won't, I have no problem going alone."

Jackie picked up her purse, pulled Jacob by the arm and drug him to the car.

When she pulled in front of her parent's home, her father was waiting for her.

Joseph, Olivia, and Jackie sat down with Jacob and explained that what he had done was very serious. He told him stories of friends in the city who were in jail for swindling. He also told him about many contractors who swindled monies from people after a hurricane that had destroyed most of the city and the people had no money left to repair their homes.

Joseph took Jacob around the block to return the money that he had stolen. He made sure he apologized to everyone.

LORD, MY CHILD
IS A CON ARTIST

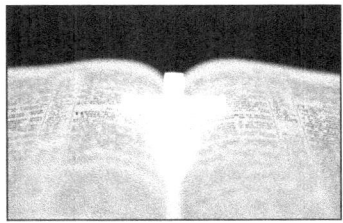

HERE IT WAS ANOTHER YEAR in middle school. Jacob rushed to case out the situation. He had to make sure that he carefully selected his seat in the classroom. He always positioned himself near Katy and Linda, the two smartest girls in the school. He had trained them well and they knew the drill. They would do the homework, and then call him with all the answers. Since his allowance from his grandparents was based on the number of A's he received, he made sure his report card was full of them. He had to work with Katy because she seemed to be a little annoyed with him toward the end of last school year. He knew he would have to talk to her and try to smooth things over. After all, he needed both of them just in case someone was absent, he could still get what he needed.

Jacob was smart – everyone at school knew it, but he just did not have any interest in proving how smart he really was. He thought to himself, "If I can continue to get those girls to take care of me, all will be well."

He walked up to Katy, "What up, ma?"

"Jacob Sawyer, I don't like it when you act like I have to help you. I don't mind helping, but you don't have to go around bragging about it to all your buddies and stuff."

"My bad, Katy, I hope you remember that the only reason I asked you and Linda to help me is because both my parents are handicapped and I spend most of my evenings taking care of them. I just told my boys that, because I did not want them to know the real reason why you are doing this."

"Well you need to be a little more considerate. If we are willing to help you, you should not be trying to make us look bad," said Katy.

"Sorry, I was just not thinking. It won't happen again, but I needed to find out if you studied for the history test next week?"

"Yes, I did."

"Katy, I don't know what I would do without you and Linda."

Jacob knew he had no intention of going over those study notes. He was busy planning his weekend. He would have to get to Linda by the end of the week so she would be prepared to position her paper so he could see her answers. He reminded himself to talk to her on Monday so she would be ready to share her paper with him.

The weekend went by very quickly. He and his dad had spent Saturday fishing and washing the cars. His dad sat with him on the bayou talking about life and how he really wanted to leave New Orleans. His dad told him that things were not going well between him and his mom and how his mom just spent all her time with church folks as if he did not matter.

Jacob already knew that the situation with his parents was bad. He could look in his mother's eyes and see that the spark was dim. It seemed that his mom spent most of her time in that spare bedroom. He often wondered what was so important about that bedroom. Jacob could see that she was disappointed in both of them. Sometimes he could hear her crying when his dad went out on Friday nights and stayed out late. He remembered a few times when his dad never came home.

Jacob loved his mom dearly, but he had decided that since he was getting older, he no longer wished to live each day making sure that she was pleased with him. After all, he had to live his life the way he wanted and sometimes other things were much more important.

Sundays were very typical in the Sawyer household. Mom made him go to church with her. His dad rarely accompanied them and would often start an argument about her making Jacob do the *church* scene. He wished she would let him stay home with his dad sometimes. He was tired of going to church. He just did not understand what the big deal was about. He was baffled as to why his mom and grandparents were so consumed by the *God* thing.

Sundays were special for two reasons. He and his mother always went out to eat with his grandparents, and then he spent the rest of the evening with his best friend, Lisa, who lived next door.

When they got home, he hurried to change his clothes, and then ran to see Lisa. He knocked on the door and she opened it with a big smile on her face. Jacob loved her like no one else. He felt so safe talking to her. She was the only one who he did not dare pretend with. After all, it wouldn't work anyway. She could always tell when he was not being honest. She was the beautiful sister he always dreamed of, but never had. She was his world and he was always going be there for her.

Lisa never attended public school. Her mom always paid for the best for her. She was in one of the most prestigious all girl schools in the city. Most of her friends were from wealthy families. Lisa had the opportunity to see the city from their eyes. She never paid attention to the drug dealers on the corner. They just did not exist in her world.

"What's up 'lil sis?" Jacob replied, as Lisa opened the door.

"Nothing much, just working on a science project. What's up with you?"

"Just going to school and chillin'. Trying to get ready for a test on Tuesday. My girls got me ready and I will be able to get all I need from Linda."

"Jacob, you are so smart, if you ever decided to use your brain instead of depending on others, you could probably be the President of the United States."

"Na, never thought about that. Maybe I will one day but, I have no intention of studying as long as I got my connection."

Lisa shut the door and walked outside. She and Jacob sat on their favorite spot under the Oak tree in front of her house. "Jacob, I know this might surprise you, but God has great things in store for you. You cannot see it now, but before it is over, you will understand why your mom and I are so passionate about our faith."

"There you go, sounding like my mama." She always says she sees things in me that God has spoken to her. I don't see any of that and when she keeps saying that it stresses me out. Why is God so interested in me? Trust me; I am trying my best to stay away from that God stuff."

"I hate to see you so frustrated; I just know I trust God to work everything out."

"Lisa, I am so glad to have you as my friend. My world is so full of phonies. It is cool talking to you because you know the *real* Jacob. I cannot talk to my parents like I can talk to you. I look into my mother's eyes and I can see that she is so disappointed in my dad and me. She never says anything, but I can tell that she is hurting. I feel bad because I never want to hurt her, but our worlds are different. She lives in that church mode all the time. It's not that I don't believe that God exists, but it don't take all that to be a Christian. I want to talk to her about it, but I just don't know where to start. I know she loves me, but there is a wall there that is as thick as concrete."

"I am glad that we are close too. I consider you to be the brother I never had. I always pray for you and thank God for having you as my brother. Your mom has developed a relationship with God that is more than you can understand right now. Someday I pray that you can find that because it will bring you so much joy and contentment to realize that someone bigger than you loves you and you love them back with all you have. It is sort of how I think marriage is like. You can open your heart to that person and it is such a safe place that you are free to love them with all your being."

"I guess I don't understand that. I can see what you mean when you talk about a man and a woman, but to feel like that about God, that is *real* deep."

"Yes, I have always admired your mom. Sometimes I stay up late at night and open my window so I can hear her pray. Listening to her has made my prayer life stronger and it has helped me to know how to pray for you. Sometimes I join her even though we are in separate houses. A prayer of agreement has more power and God knows when we are praying together for you and your dad. Your mom loves the both of you and all she wants is for you to be close again and serve God together."

"I know that is what she wants, but I feel sorry for her because my dad and I are not feeling this *Jesus* thing. If I could just find a way to connect with her as my mother, I think that it would make both of us happy."

"Have you thought about trying to talk to her about this?"

"I did try one time, but it did not turn out good. Seems like it just made her more frustrated."

"When you feel the time is right, approach her again. I will pray you have a better outcome next time."

"Man, what if it makes things worse?"

"Jacob, you just don't understand what it's like to trust God for things you cannot see, but I know He wants this for you too. You will have to just go with your heart and He will do the rest."

"This is weird to me. You know I don't let people in my head. I definitely can't see room in there for God."

"Jacob I promise you, He will do it if you just give Him a chance."

"Okay, how will I know when the time is right?"

"You will know; you will feel it in your gut."

"Alright, I will let you know when it happens."

They hugged each other and went inside to prepare for school the next day.

When Jacob got off the bus on Monday, he ran down the hallway to look for Linda. He had to make sure that she was ready to support him during the test on Tuesday.

"Hey Linda, can I holler at you for a minute?" He made sure to greet everyone surrounding them. After all, he could not take a chance at having his cover blown.

He found her in the hallway talking to two other girls. It seemed that everyone found time to be in the company of Katy and Linda.

Jacob realized he might not have been the only one needing small favors. Jacob could see that Linda and Katy had made the homework thing a profitable venue and was getting money for copies of their homework from everyone. He thought to himself, thank God they feel sorry for me and I don't have to pay for their help.

Linda walked toward him then replied, "Hey Jacob, what's up with you?

"Well I was just checking with you about the test tomorrow.

Please make sure you tilt your paper to the right so I can see your answers?"

In a concerned tone, Linda responded. "Will do. Just be careful because Ms. Johnson caught Cedric cheating on her math exam and he got an "F" on his grade along with detention."

"I'll be extra careful. Cannot afford to get in trouble."

"I know. See you later."

When Tuesday came, Jacob made sure to walk to school a little earlier than normal. He needed to look at that study guide just for a little while. He knew he should have gotten to it before now, but he was not worried because Linda had his back. He pulled out the guide and began to view it. He could not believe how much information was on that guide. There was no way he would be able to cram any of this in this morning. He thought to himself, Katy and Linda really make my life easier; I will have to get them something special for Christmas.

As Ms. Crenshaw began handing out the test papers he paid special attention to Linda and how she was seated.

"Students please make sure your name is at the top of each sheet and I must caution you, I will be watching carefully and cheaters will be severely punished."

Jacob looked at the paper as she handed it to him. He was shocked to see that it was three pages long. He read the questions and realized that he did not know any of the answers. It would take a lot to be able to retrieve all this information from Linda. He regretted not looking at the study guide over the weekend.

Linda was good. She had positioned her paper just right. She finished page one quickly and turned the paper to the second page, and Jacob was missing two answers at the bottom of the page. He dropped his pencil trying to get her attention, but this did not work. He got so distracted; he did not notice Ms. Crenshaw watching his every move.

As he turned to page two, he did not see that Ms. Crenshaw was standing over him. He looked over at Linda and waited for the opportunity to get the answer. Katy saw the whole thing and knew that he was in trouble. As he began to right the answer down, Ms. Crenshaw took his paper.

"Jacob please see me after class is over."

His heart sank. He had to figure out how to get out of this one. He thought to himself. Did she really see me? Should I admit to cheating?

He decided to wait and see what she said, and then he would know how to respond.

When class ended, he picked up his backpack and walked to her desk.

"Jacob I saw your eyes wandering towards Linda's desk and I need to make sure that you have answered these questions on your own before I allow you to finish this test. I see you have answered question number 1 with the name of Abraham Lincoln. Can you tell me a little about the Gettysburg Address?

"No, Ms. Crenshaw, I really don't know much about it. I did look on Linda's paper for the answers. I have been so swamped with family matters lately, that I did not get enough time to study."

"Well, I am sure you know that cheating is an automatic "F."

"I know, I will definitely have to do better if I am going to pass this course."

Yes, you will, but that is not the only thing you will have to resolve. I will be reporting this to the office and your parents will be notified.

"Ms. Crenshaw, please don't contact my parents, they have enough to deal with right now. They are not in the best of health and I am afraid they are about to get a divorce."

"Jacob, if you were that concerned about upsetting your parents, you would have been doing your best to get your schoolwork done, instead of cheating and trying to get by."

"You are right, Ms. Crenshaw, it would just kill me if I made things worse at home." Is there any way I can do punish work to make up for this?"

"No, I cannot have any student thinking they can cheat on my test and get away with it. I will think this over tonight and let you know what my decision is tomorrow."

"Thank you, Ms. Crenshaw. It won't happen again."

Jacob rushed home to talk to Lisa. She could help him figure out what to do. He knew he had made a mess of things. She always kept him grounded and he needed her to help him make things right.

He rang the doorbell and no one answered. As he turned his head, he saw his mother's car turning the corner. Jacob was surprised because it was rare for her to get home so early. His dad had worked overtime the past few days, so he knew was probably just getting out of bed.

Jacob had a lump in his throat. He definitely did not want to go home before he talked to Lisa.

"Jacob, could you come home for a minute? I need to talk to you."

Just the tone of his mother's voice made him know that this was not good.

They walked inside together and found his dad in the kitchen making a sandwich.

"Donald, I rushed home after getting a call from Ms. Crenshaw. It appears that Jacob was cheating on his history exam today."

As he looked in his mother's eyes he could see how disappointed she was. Jacob always had trouble dealing with disappointing her. If she only knew how much he really cherished her, she would find a way to reassure him that he was still the apple of her eye.

"I am sorry, but that test was so long and I just did not have enough time to study it all."

"Jacob, I am so disappointed in you; please don't make things worse by giving me excuses. You did not open a book this past weekend. How do you think you can pass without giving your schoolwork a priority? You are relieved of a lot of household chores during the school year in order to make sure that you have time for your studies."

"I don't know what to say, I've just been goofing off lately."

"Well I can tell you this; some things are going to change around here. You will not be getting your allowance for two weeks, your chores will resume and I had better not see a report card with anything less than a "C" on it.

His dad just stood there. He knew his son needed to be punished, but he was tired of Jackie making them feel that they were failures.

"Jackie, don't make more of this than need be. Jacob knows he is wrong. We do not need to beat him down to a pulp with our words."

"Donald, there you go again, excusing things that need to be addressed. That is why our son is always going around manipulating everything and everybody in order to get what he wants. It is time for him to begin accepting responsibility for his actions. I am trying to make him be responsible and you make me out to be the bad guy."

Jacob looked in his dad's eyes and he knew that he was losing it. Then his dad rushed over to the cabinet where his mother was standing and began screaming.

"Jackie, don't say another word! You think you are the only one who is disappointed? You walk around here with your *holier than thou attitude* and you think you are the only one hurting. Don't talk about my son, and don't talk about me! I am sick of it! You need to get real and stop being so judgmental!"

Jacob began to cry. He could not believe that his cheating had made his dad act this way with his mother. He knew in his heart that she did not deserve this.

"Stop it, please. I cannot stand to see you all like this! For you to argue like this over my grades makes me think that your problems are my fault. You think I cannot see that you all hate each other? How do you think that makes me feel? I see both of you walking around here every day and all I see is hostility. What has happened to us? We used to have fun. We used to be happy. I am so tired of the pretense. You think I am motivated to do school work? All my mind can see is that my parents are about to get a divorce. There it is! I said it! The big 'D' word. Stop faking it! I cannot stand living in this house."

His mother started crying. She had no idea that Jacob could tell that they were having problems. She spent many nights in a cold bed, wishing that Donald would just hold her. But somehow, he would flinch if her skin just happened to brush against his.

"Jacob, I did not know that you had been so worried about us."

"Your dad and I are having problems, but it has nothing to do with you. Donald, we need to consider getting counseling." I can call my pastor to make an appointment if that is okay with you."

"If you think I am going to set foot in that church, you have lost your mind. If I agree to counseling, it will be with someone I choose."

Jackie responded, "Okay, that's fine with me. Wednesday evenings is best for me."

"I will set it up and let you know."

"Alright."

CHAPTER TEN

GOD, THIS CANNOT BE HAPPENING

THINGS AT HOME HAD GOTTEN WORSE than ever. Jacob had begun to study and do all his chores. His mom and dad had begun seeing a marriage counselor, but it seemed that it was making his dad angrier. He could see how harmful it was for his parents to have pretended for so long. There was a cold atmosphere throughout the house and it was not good. His dad spent more nights away from home and his mother spent more time in that room. Jacob could see that she was losing weight. He knew that was because she had been fasting so much.

He thought to himself, God, I know you have no reason to listen to me, but if You care about my mother like she cares about You, You would help her. He knew he had to talk to Lisa about it. After all, she always gave him good advice.

He ran out the front door. He had to get to her before dark or he would have to wait until the next day.

As he knocked on the door, Lisa rushed out. She knew that things were bad between Jacob's parents. She could hear his mother's prayers and they were prayers of desperation. She knew when his dad had stayed out all night because his mom would spend the night in her prayer room.

"Hey Lisa, got a minute?"

"Sure, what's up?"

"Well, everything at home is falling apart. Remember, I told you that I got caught cheating on that history test and when I got home my parents got in a big argument over it. Well, a year has passed since then and although they have been seeing a marriage counselor, it seems that things are worse than before."

"I know that things are bad. I have been hearing your mother's prayers at night. Sometimes she is in her prayer room all night."

"I know. Lisa, I cannot stand to see my mom like this. Have you seen how much weight she has lost?" I don't know what to do."

"Have you prayed about it?"

"Me? Well, I don't know if you would call it a prayer, but I did ask God to help my mom. I know He probably would not entertain anything I said, so I asked him to do it for her sake."

"Well, we can pray together, but you have to come to God believing that He is God, not some figment of your imagination."

"I do believe in God, I just have a hard time trusting in someone I cannot touch."

"I know you go to church with your mother, but if you are having trouble trusting in God, then maybe you are having trouble believing in Him, too. You probably have given thought to what you have been taught about God, but you may not believe that He is *who* He says He is. Think about it like this. You place your trust in a chair that it will hold you and then you just sit down on it. When you walk in front of the chair, you can no longer see it; however, you know the chair is behind you. That is why you have no problem sitting down, because you trust that it is there and that it can hold you. It is the same way with *really* believing God. You know He is with you, even though you cannot see Him and because you know He is there, you can trust Him.

"I see people like this all the time. They go to church, and they quote scriptures all day long, but when it boils down to it, their belief system is faulty. I am not trying to be judgmental – God just needs all of us to be honest with Him and say what is really on our heart, not what is in our head. You know there is a verse in the Bible where a man came to Jesus and asked him *if* he could heal his son. Jesus scolded him for using the word *if,* then the man said, 'I believe, but help my unbelief.' He was willing to be honest with God and admit that he was having trouble. His head knew it, but his heart was in a different place.

"You see, Jacob, as long as we keep speaking from our head and not from our heart, we are limiting God by not giving Him permission to touch our wounded place. He knows our human condition. He knows we are hurting. He knows what is really on our heart, but if we deny what is there, He will not help us. Do you understand what I am saying?"

"Yes, I get it. I never realized that I was struggling to believe God. I really need to get to a place where I can reach out to Him. My mom needs me to pray for her. After all, she has prayed for my dad and me all this time."

"Jacob, I really believe you need to go to your mom and talk to her about this. You have got to trust her and open up to her. She loves you and would welcome a 'real' conversation."

"Okay. I will"

Jacob hugged Lisa. He felt so much better.

"Thanks, sis."

"You are welcome anytime."

He ran inside. He now had the courage to approach his mother. He was not going to put this off any longer. He had to do it tonight. His dad was not home and this was the perfect time.

When he walked inside he gave his mother a kiss.

"Jacob, have you eaten yet?"

"No, mama."

"Well come on, I will fix your plate so you can eat and then get your homework done."

"Mama, can we sit to the table together like we used to? I would love to talk to you."

His mom was shocked, but excited. She had missed her long conversations with her son. She did not like the place they were in. It was as if they were total strangers.

"Son, I am so happy that you want to talk. I have missed our time together. I have been praying for God to bring us closer."

"Mama, I have struggled so long feeling like you did not understand me. I know you grew up around the church folks, but it is different for me. My life is not like yours. My friends are not like yours. I don't know many people like you and my grandparents. Everybody I know sees life differently. When you look at me, I can sense that you are disappointed and this hurts. I feel like you are sorry for having me. I never want to see you in pain, especially if it looks like I am the one who is causing it. That's why I spend most of my time at my friends and only come home at curfew."

Jacob's mother started to cry.

"Mama, please don't cry. I cannot take it when you cry."

"Jacob, I have to tell you the truth. I am most disappointed in myself, not you. I have not regretted for one minute that God gave you to me. Do you remember when I told you the story about my dream of having a child and God told me to call him Jacob? Well, I have felt guilty throughout my marriage because I did not consult God when I decided to marry your dad. I may have rushed to get married before your dad was really ready. I feel that everything is my fault, not your's or your dad's. My mother tried to warn me about rushing into marriage, but I wouldn't listen. Now look at the turmoil it has caused you, having two parents with different positions about how to exercise their faith. You are right; I did not grow up like that. No matter what was going on around me, home provided me with a strong foundation and example of what it was like to trust God with all my heart. I cannot imagine what it is like for you to live with your dad and I being at odds about something as critical as our beliefs."

"I know that your childhood was different, but I live what I live. The only person I know who thinks like you is Lisa, but I don't feel that she is looking down on me. I can see that she accepts me where I am now. Mama, I just need you to understand that things are different for me. Just keep praying mama. One day I just might get there."

"Jacob, I will never give up on you. I will try harder to let you know that I understand where you are. I do get frustrated, but I am not condemning you, just the situation. I will try harder to be more understanding. Please forgive me if you thought for a minute that I was disappointed in you."

Jacob hugged his mother so tightly. It felt good to have her warm embrace. He remembered the days when she could comfort him like no one else.

They both looked at each other as they heard the key turn in the front door.

Jacob looked into his father's eyes and he knew that he had been drinking.

"What's up, daddy?"

"Hello son, I need to speak to your mother for a minute, do you mind?"

"No problem, I'll just run outside and shoot a few hoops in the back yard."

As he proceeded to go out the back door, he had this uneasiness. He really did not feel like playing ball at all.

It was not long before he could hear the arguing outside the door. He stood at the door and tried to listen.

His father was doing most of the screaming.

"Jackie, there is nothing you can do to convince me to stay! Hopefully, I can find someone who makes me feel like I am still alive. I hope you can find a *preacher man* to make you happy, too!"

Jackie rushed over to Donald. She was so angry she began to shake him.

"Get your hands off me Jackie!"

Jackie knew that losing her temper was not the right response. She was frustrated that Donald was blind to the fact that she loved him more than life itself. She walked away in silence, knowing that his mind was made up and there was nothing she could do about it.

Jacob ran inside. The thing he had feared the most had now become a reality.

"Pop, don't touch her!"

Donald pried Jackie's hands from his arms and turned toward Jacob.

"Son, we need to talk."

"You don't need to say a thing to me, man," shouted Jacob. I already heard. I can't believe you would just leave us like this!"

Jacob gave his father a piercing look. He wanted him to know that he was angry. He could not see how he could ever forgive his dad for this.

"Pop, you are only thinking about yourself! You cannot possibly care how you are hurting us!"

"Son, I know this is difficult. I don't want you to think for a minute that I am abandoning you. Things between you and I don't have to change; we will just be living in two different houses. I am not far away. You can come over whenever you want."

"What makes you think I want to come over? I heard my mother crying. When you hurt her, you hurt me!" I do not want to be bothered with you anymore. I can take care of my mother all by myself!"

"Jacob, you don't mean what you're saying. I will talk to you when you calm down."

"Forget it, pop!"

As his dad walked out the door, all Jacob could think about was how he had prayed and how this *God* had disappointed him.

"God, are you real? I gave You a chance to show me what You are about and this is what I get?"

He thought to himself. This *Jesus* thing must all be a big joke. I just need to go back to what I know, Jacob being in control of his own world.

Jackie was sitting at the kitchen table crying with her head down.

"Mama, please don't cry. I can take care of us. I am so upset with this *God thing*. I almost feel that He is making you hurt because of me, and if that's the way He treats people, what good is He anyway?"

Jackie raised her head from the table and Jacob could see the fury in her eyes.

"Jacob don't you dare blame God for what is going on in this household."

"Why shouldn't I blame him? Do you know I said a prayer because Lisa suggested I pray for you and daddy? Now look at what has happened. It is as if I never prayed at all. I will never put myself in the position to trust in 'this God' that you are always praying to. Mama you spend most of your time in that prayer room and it has done you no good."

"Jacob, you cannot blame God for this. Your dad chose to leave. God does not force anyone to do the right thing. He gives us all freewill to choose what we want. If you want to blame anyone, you can blame your father, not God."

"Well I tell you what; I am not feeling this *trusting God* thing, because if you say He is interested in *my* freewill, I *will* not trust Him. How about that?"

Jacob stormed off. He definitely was not interested in continuing a conversation about her God.

As he hurried to his room, he thought to himself, I guess I will be the subject of her prayers tonight.

Jackie could not wait until the house quieted down. She was desperate for God to comfort her, as only He could do. Her life was totally out of control.

It was as if she felt herself running into the room to meet with Him. She collapsed to the floor, tears streaming down her face. She thought to herself, although I have been fasting and praying, I need to share my troubles with the ladies in my mother's prayer group. She was always taught the power of prayers of agreement. She could hear Ms. Hattie's words, *One can put a thousand to flight, and two can put 10,000 to flight.* The enemy had waged an all out war against her family. She felt her strength waning. If she had not needed it before, she knew she now needed the ladies to cover her in prayer. She decided to call her mother in the morning and arrange for a special prayer meeting. She never made it to her bedroom that night, she knew God had not forsaken her; she just needed to trust him for a miracle.

CHAPTER ELEVEN

Yield Not
To Temptation

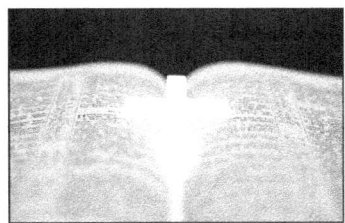

Donald had rented an apartment in the Pontchartrain Beach Apartments. He had gotten a two-bedroom apartment with hopes that Jacob would agree to spend the night sometimes. However, it was obvious that they were a long way away from having any father-son sleepovers.

He had furnished the apartment modestly with only the necessities. After all, he wanted to make sure there were enough monies left for him to give to Jackie. He had wanted to move out for a long time, but somehow, there was no cause for celebration.

As he dosed off to sleep, he realized that he needed to take some time getting used to not having a warm body next to him. He also knew he would miss the wonderful meals he had at home. Since he was not a cook, he would have to figure out what to eat. He was concerned because if he chose to eat out, then it would take most of his monthly budget.

The first week in his apartment was rather insignificant. He managed to find things in the freezer section of the grocery to heat in the microwave. He had gone by the home twice during the week to try to talk to Jacob, but he was unsuccessful. Donald had decided to drown himself in his work in order to help him cope. He managed to work twenty hours of overtime that week, which had kept him from drinking.

Well, it was now Friday night, time for the usual routine. As Donald got dressed, this night felt different to him. For one, he had no one to answer to. He could stay out all night if he wanted and not feel bad. He knew Bridget would be there and he was looking forward to dancing the night away. He knew he had to be careful, though. He was vulnerable and he knew it.

He had been meeting up with Bridget at the jazz club for a while now. He told her he was married, so they had not had any other contact. However, every Friday they would look for each other, and then they would drink and dance the night away. He especially enjoyed the slow dances. She always smelled good and between her and the alcohol, he could almost forget what was going on at home. He thought to himself, I can't let her know that I have moved out. If I let myself be vulnerable and make any advances, it will only make matters worse.

As he got into the club, the first person he saw was his friend Roland. They laughed and joked with each other. Roland was also separated from his family. Donald knew that the Friday night excursions had created a problem for Ronald, yet here he was in the same place. Roland had been in his apartment for over a year now, and it had become a place where he always took a woman home on Friday nights. Truth be told, Roland had gotten the apartment before they separated in order to have a place to take women. Although Donald was now separated from Jackie, he had no intention of following in Roland's footsteps and bringing women over. He was still married, and he intended to stay that way, for now.

By the time he saw Bridget, he had already had a few drinks. He bought drinks for their table and they began dancing. In the past,

Bridget had been careful not to ask him about home, because it was obvious he did not want to talk about it. Somehow tonight, he was like a broken record. He told her about them separating, about Jacob being angry and not wanting to have anything to do with him. Before he knew it, he had shared that he was now living in the Pontchartrain Beach Apartments. Afterwards, he could not realize he had said all of that. It was now three a.m. and he was tired. He said his goodbye's and he drove home.

No sooner than he put his jacket down, the doorbell rang. He looked through the peephole and saw it was Bridget. Fear gripped him, immediately.

Regrettably, he opened the door.

"Hello Donald," Bridget replied. "Just came by to bring you a housewarming gift."

"Thank you, Bridget," Donald said, as she pushed her way past him.

She had music piped in on her phone. She had a bottle of wine and two glasses.

"Donald, as you were talking about your family tonight, I could see that you were really bothered about things. Just thought you could use a little cheering up."

She poured the wine, sat the glasses on the coffee table and sat down.

"Yes," Donald replied, "this is all new to me."

They began to talk. She made him laugh. Then all of a sudden, she started kissing him. She kissed him on his neck. Donald knew he was in trouble, but he kept quiet and let her continue. Before he knew it, he was kissing her back. Then she started unbuttoning his shirt. His heart wanted her to stop, but his mind wanted her to keep going.

All of a sudden Donald found strength he did not know he had.

"I am sorry Bridget, I can't do this. My life is already complicated. I don't want to complicate things anymore."

"Come on Donald. I see how lonely you are. I just want you to forget your troubles."

"I am sorry Bridget. You need to leave."

"I understand, you are obviously not ready. I'll see you on next Friday"

As he closed the door behind her, he felt sick. This experience was so troubling to him that he began to throw up. However, he knew that he was rescued from a major catastrophe. Having someone come onto him like that and the fact that it caused him to throw up, made him realize how much he still loved his wife. He thought about Jackie and all her prayers. He thought to himself, she had prayed him through a major attack from the enemy.

CHAPTER TWELVE

FROM BAD TO WORSE

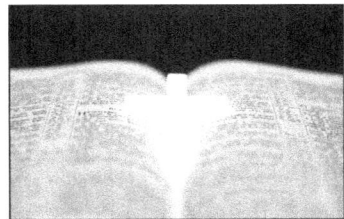

WELL THERE WAS AN OLD WIVE'S TALE which said that time would heal all wounds. Jackie had firsthand knowledge that this was exactly that – a wive's tale.

Jacob was now in his senior year in high school.

Things continued to be strained between Jacob and his dad. He would come over and Jacob hardly spoke.

This disconnect between he and his father really hurt, but he refused to give his father any inkling about how he felt.

Lisa was the most important person in his life. They were both graduating and she was going off to college on a full scholarship. He was concerned about Lisa, though. She had befriended a guy that Jacob knew was not in her league. Since Jacob spent most of his days on the streets, he knew what was going on and he did not think Lisa had a clue about this guy. He had tried to talk to her about him once before, but she was not listening. When Lisa made up her mind about someone, or something, it was hard to get through to her. Jacob had seen this guy on the corner with the most dangerous guys in the neighborhood. He approached him to try and get him to stay away from Lisa, but this ended in him getting punched.

As Jacob walked to Lisa's house, he was trying to figure out a way to convince her to stay away from this loser. He was dangerous and Lisa had to understand how dangerous he was.

He knocked on the door and she answered it.

"What happened to you?" Lisa was alarmed to see that Jacob had a bloody nose.

"I saw your boyfriend and told him to stay away from you and he punched me in the face. Lisa, please ditch this loser, he is trouble."

"Jacob if you would stop thinking you have to manage my friends, you would not be having these kinds of problems. He is not my boyfriend, he is just a friend. I told you not to worry about me so much. Somebody has to try to reach him and show him a better way."

"Lisa, he is dangerous. You don't have any idea what he is doing out there on that corner."

"Jacob, I am not as naïve as you think I am. I know what is happening on that corner, but if everybody tip toes around these guys in constant fear, who will reach them?"

Jacob stormed away. "Okay Lisa, don't say I didn't warn you."

As the year progressed, Jacob decided to try to befriend these guys. After all, he had to know what they were up to if he was going to protect Lisa.

Jacob walked up to Jonathan. "What's up bro?"

"Man these streets are hot. At this rate, I can make my million before I turn twenty. Once I make my money, I am getting away from here and you won't see me in this part of town. Man you need to think about my offer to you. You are so smart; you could have this whole neighborhood wrapped around your little finger."

"Man, my mama would kill me. She has all these pipe dreams about me going to college and being a lawyer. I have no interest in college, I just want to finish high school then I will try to start my own business."

"Man, what type of business are you planning on?"

"I have two friends at my school who are rappers. I would love to produce their music."

"I tell you what, work with me for six months and I will front everything you need to get started. In fact, I'll hook you up with this guy who has a recording studio and he could probably record it for you."

"Man that's what's up, I'll think about it and get back to you. Since my dad has left, it would definitely help if I had finances to help my mom."

Jacob said his goodbye's and began walking home.

He thought to himself, maybe Jonathan is not that bad after all! He was offering Jacob an opportunity to really pursue his dream. Jacob thought to himself, he had to make this last month in school meaningful. He would create his business plan, and if he could not find any other way to fund it, he might just take Jonathan up on his offer.

Graduation went off without a hitch. His dad had attended but Jacob still wanted nothing to do with him.

Although Jackie was happy to see her son graduate, she was disappointed that his circle of friends had changed and she did not approve of his company. It did not appear that any of these guys had any aspirations. She was also disappointed that she could not convince him to go to college. He finally agreed to would enroll at Bordeaux Community College in the spring.

As the summer progressed, Jacob became more involved with Jonathan and his crew. He was a quick study as he learned the business. He was good at following instructions and made sure that no one violated their territory.

Lisa had a month before she left for school. He had to remain incognito until she was gone. He could not bear for her to know he had joined the drug scene. Truth be told, he was frightened at the thought of her leaving him. Who would he turn to then? Who could he pour his heart out to without worrying about being judged? No one but Lisa loved him like that.

Well the time had come for her to leave. Jacob had decided to avoid her. Saying goodbye was something he could not muster up the courage to do. He was also worried that she would figure out what he was doing. After all, she had the canny ability to sometimes read his thoughts. So he made ridiculous excuses and waited for her to be gone. As her mother's car drove off, he began to dial her number.

"Hello sis, sorry I missed you."

"Jacob Sawyer, why are you avoiding me?"

"Just got a lot on my mind and a lot to do. Your mom said you were coming home for the Labor Day weekend, I promise we will hook up then, okay."

"Alright Jacob, but you have been scaring me lately. What is going on, you have got to be up to something."

Jacob replied, "I am good, don't worry about me, I got this."

"I know you, Jacob. When you say that, it is just the opposite. You can't fool me. God has uniquely connected us and He lets me know when you are in trouble and I can see that you are *definitely* in a bad place."

"Go do 'you,' Lisa. I got me."

"Yeah, right, I will see you when I get home for Labor Day weekend."

Lisa had this funny feeling. She was deeply troubled by her friends tone and demeanor lately. As they drove down the highway, she began to pray silently. *God please protect Jacob. I can see his heart has become so hard. I trust you to get his attention.*

Although he avoided Lisa, he was not able to avoid his mother. She had become more and more frustrated with him and his late night excursions, her seeing him on that corner had taken a toll on her. She had prayed and fasted, but she knew that God would not violate Jacob's will. Until his desires for life changed, all she could do was pray.

Jackie knew that the time had come for her to confront her son. She was ready and it was time to have an all out war with the enemy of his soul. She knew she had to fight. She had to tell him that she knew what he was about. He had to know that she would not tolerate his behavior any longer.

It was two o'clock in the morning and he was nowhere to be found. Suddenly she heard the key turn in the front door lock.

"Son, I know what you are doing and I am not pleased with it. I never thought that I would see the day when you would have chosen such a dangerous, ungodly lifestyle. I cannot sit by quietly while you gradually self destruct. If you are going to live here, you are going to have to get your life in order."

Jackie began to cry. She had already lost Donald, although she thought she thought she could pray him through his struggles. Now she was losing her son to the streets. She could not bear the pain. She remembered her dream. What about God's promise to change him?

Seeing his mother cry made Jacob angry, not with his mother, but with God Himself.

"Mama I feel sorry for you. You have spent your whole life depending on a God who has let you down every time. Yet, you think that I am going to give Him control over my life, it just won't happen. I know He does not care about me, but the least He could do is be as devoted to you as you are to Him. He has failed you and I will never forget that. I am moving on. I am making my own way, living my life like I want to live it. At least I know what to expect in the streets. At least I am not living my life depending on someone who *cannot* and *will not* help me."

Jackie began screaming. "Jacob don't you say another blasphemous word!"

"Mama I know this may hurt but I am not you. I want no part of your life! I want no part of your God! At the end of the day, I have to be true to me. I am grown now. I won't step foot into your church any more. Don't waste your time praying for me, it won't change a thing. I have no desire to live like you."

Jacob picked up his backpack and started walking towards the door.

Her voice became faint, as she could no longer hold back the tears. "Jacob, please come back. Please don't leave!"

Jacob opened the door and turned back toward his mother. "Mama I do not mean to hurt you, but you have got to let me live my life."

Jackie fell to the floor sobbing profusely. She did not know what else to do. She knew the women in the prayer group had been praying for her. Her mother had been updating them on everything that had been going on. She had even told them about her dream about Jacob and that God was going to change his heart. No matter what things looked like, she just had to believe that God would do what he said he would do. She did not sleep that night. As she lay on the floor in the prayer room, her favorite Tamala Mann song came to her mind and she began to sing:

Take me to the king,

I don't have much to bring,

My heart is torn in pieces,

It's my offering,

Take me to the throne,

Leave me there alone,

To gaze upon your glory

And to sing to You this song

Jackie had become weary. She did not have any strength to pray. She just lay there. She knew that when her strength failed, the Holy Spirit was capable of praying through her. God knows she had not been a perfect parent, but she had tried her best to show Jacob what was right. She had to trust God to do the rest.

She lay before the Lord as the words began to flow:

"Father, please forgive me for beating Jacob over the head with scriptures. Pour out Your Spirit upon him. Speak to Jacob, and help him to *really* hear You. Help him to recognize Your voice. Open his ears to hear the truth and resist all the lies that the world has spoken to him. Please draw him back into Your loving arms. Convert his heart and bring him back to You. When he returns to You, shower him with Your love and never let him go. You are his *first* parent. You can do more with him than I could ever do. Give him a hip changing experience, just like Jacob. Cause him to acknowledge his evil ways. Create a new heart, and renew a right spirit within him. Transform him into Your image. Amen."

Jackie fell fast to sleep and before she knew it, morning had come and it was time to go to work.

CHAPTER THIRTEEN

HOLDING ON
WHEN LIFE MAKES NO SENSE

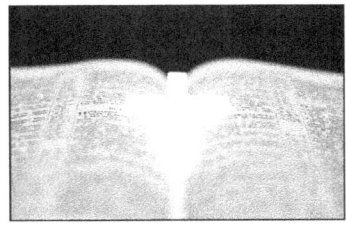

THE NEXT FEW WEEKS were difficult as she watched Jacob come in and out of the house during the middle of the night. He rarely said much to her and she knew that prayer was her only weapon. She was certain that trying to talk to him would only make matters worse.

Labor Day weekend was approaching and Jackie knew that Lisa was coming home. She figured that he would spend more time with her and less time in the streets. She prayed that Lisa would be able to talk some sense in Jacob.

The weekend was finally here and Lisa could not wait to get home.

She had hitched a ride with some friends and was in route to New Orleans. Her phone rang; she looked at the number and answered.

"Hello Jonathan, how have you been?"

She had not spoken to him in a while and wanted to play catch up.

Jonathan replied, I am good, how are you?"

"I have really been praying for you, Jonathan. I was hoping you were close to making some decisions about your future. I know that God has so much more for your life than you can see right now."

"I know you care about me Lisa, and I know I need to make some changes, it's just not time yet. Hope we can get together to chat when you get in town."

"Well, I didn't get a chance to see Jacob before I left for school. I am hopeful I can catch up with him tonight. Maybe we can get together on Saturday."

"Okay, peace out."

She thought about the night Jonathan opened up to her about his childhood. How he told her both his parents were on drugs and they rarely had food to eat. He said they never missed a day of school because that was often their only meal. He said the weekends were tough with no food in the house. Since he was the oldest, he used to go to the corner grocery, looking for things that had been thrown out. Sometimes he was lucky enough to get enough food for the whole weekend. Then, when he was about nine, this drug dealer started giving him money for food. Before he knew it, he had more money than he could imagine, all he had to do was make a few runs for him. When his dad realized he had cash, he beat him up and took all of it. He ran from the house and never returned. Now he says the streets are his family. Lisa could see that Jonathan had a good heart; he was just the victim of his circumstances.

She knew she could not let herself be distracted. She had to get to Jacob as soon as possible. She began to dial his number. She was not going to let him get away from her this time.

The phone rang and immediately rolled over to his recording. She had to talk to him. She was not going to take no for an answer.

"Jacob Sawyer, you will not get away from me this weekend. Call me as soon as you get this message."

Jacob looked down at his phone. He knew he would have to see Lisa; he just had no idea what to say. He dialed Jonathan's number. He needed him to keep Lisa occupied while he made a run."

"Hey man, what's up?"

"I just got a call from Lisa. I have been avoiding her, because I did not want her to know what I am into."

"Yeah, I just spoke to her a few minutes ago. She is waiting to see you."

"I know, but I have a few loose ends to tie up before I can head that way. I need a huge favor; can you go by there to keep her company until I get there?"

"Man, that's what's up. I just called Lisa, because I wanted to see her, but she really wants to see you. I will go by and run interference until you can get to her."

"Thanks man, I really appreciate it."

"No problem. I will be so happy to see her."

Jonathan walked up as Lisa got out the car. She gave him a hug and he helped her get her bags out the car.

They walked inside together. Lisa's mother was in the kitchen cooking her favorite meal.

As Jonathan watched, Lisa gave her mother a warm embrace. He could see how much they loved each other. Watching them made a lump swell up in his throat. He wished he had had a mother like that. He now understood why Lisa was such a loving, giving person. He knew that her unconditional love toward him had softened him a bit. He wondered what he would have been like if he had lived in a house like this.

Jonathan and Lisa walked back outside and they sat under their favorite tree.

"So how is life at school?"

"College is a lot of work, if you want to do well; you definitely cannot get caught up in the party scene."

"Lisa, I have to tell you how much you have influenced me. I watched you with your mother. I have never seen that before. You actually love each other. I wish I had a family like yours."

As Jonathan turned his head, he saw this car speeding up to them and it concerned him. He was wondering if the neighborhood gang was up to something. He decided it was best for them to get back inside.

"Lisa, can we go back inside? That car is making me uncomfortable." As they began walking toward the front door, the car sped up and began to shoot.

A bullet hit Jonathan in the leg and he fell. As Lisa stooped down to help him, a round of bullets went straight to her head.

Just as Jonathan began to scream for Lisa's mom, the car sped off.

Lisa's mother ran out the door to find her daughter in a pool of blood. She picked her up and held her.

"Breathe, baby, breathe. Help is on the way!"

There was a gurgle in her breathing. She knew what that sounded like. She never forgot that sound when her husband took his last breath.

She began to cry. "God this cannot be happening! I cannot lose my little girl! She is all I have since You took Ronald from me! There is nothing else left to my life!"

With blood covering her, she continued to rock her child. Then she heard it. Her final breath had come. She continued to rock her as she sobbed like there was no tomorrow.

Jonathan was in shock, he had to get someone to help. He looked next door and saw Jackie's car.

He crawled to the front door and raised his body to ring the bell.

Jackie opened the door and immediately saw Jonathan on the ground. As she was about to stoop over to help him up, he cried, "Ms. Sawyer, Lisa is badly hurt, please call for an ambulance."

Jackie ran next door. She saw Lisa on the ground and her mother was holding her. She screamed as she pulled her cell phone from her pocket to dial 911. "God please help us!"

She put her arms around Lisa and her mother and they both sobbed until the police and ambulance came.

Jackie followed the ambulance to the hospital. She was still in shock. Where was Jacob?

She called her friend Lynn and she met them at the hospital. All of Lisa's extended family had shown up and they were all devastated. Jackie prayed that God would give her the strength to be there for Lisa's mother. She could not imagine the depth of her pain.

Jonathan had been treated for a bullet that had grazed his leg, and then he was released.

Jackie was uncomfortable with Jonathan. She knew he had had a bad influence on her son, but she was grateful that they did not have to deal with two dead bodies.

CHAPTER FOURTEEN

How Can This be?

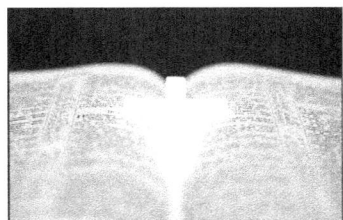

The day was almost done and Jacob had one more stop to make. The last run had been rather difficult. This dude insisted that he did not owe the amount Jonathan had quoted to him. He threatened to kill both he and Jonathan. Jacob calmed him down by telling him he would have to take this up with Jonathan.

He had just turned onto St. Raymond Avenue. All of a sudden, someone pulled up on side of him and began shooting. Jacob could feel blood running down his legs. He knew both his legs had been hit. He began speeding to try and get away. He had not moved fast enough though because he heard six shots hit his car. One bullet had shot through the knuckle on his left hand. Another bullet was lodged in his cell phone which was in the driver door pocket. He saw another bullet heading toward his temple. He could hear the sound of it piercing the glass, and then all of a sudden the bullet was nowhere to be found. It was as if someone or something had caught it.

There was blood coming from his stomach and he did not know how serious this injury was. He just knew he had to do everything he could to make it to the hospital.

He drove as fast as he could toward the East Orleans Hospital. He made it to the emergency room. There was a man outside smoking a cigarette. Jacob could not roll down his driver window, nor could he open the door since the bullets had destroyed the motor and the lock. He was able to get the back left window down and he began to holler for help.

As the man came toward him, Jacob told him he had been shot and asked him to help him get out the passenger door. The man told him to sit still while he got help.

The hospital staff came out with a stretcher and pulled him from the car.

Jackie was still at the hospital with Lisa's family when she heard her phone ring.

She answered, "Hello."

"May I please speak to Mrs. Jackie Sawyer?"

"Speaking."

"Ma'am, I am a nurse at East Orleans Hospital. I am calling you because your son, Jacob is in the emergency room. He has been shot."

Jackie threw the phone down and fell to the floor. It was more than she could take.

"No, God, no!"

Thank God, Lynn was with her and she picked up the phone.

The nurse proceeded to explain that none of Jacob's injuries were life threatening, but that he would be in the hospital for a few days to treat his injuries and prevent infection from setting in. Lynn thanked the nurse and told her that they were on their way. The hospital staff were standing over Jackie because she had blacked out for a minute. Lynn explained to them what had happened and that she had to take Jackie to East Orleans Hospital to see about Jacob. When they got in the car, Lynn proceeded to call Donald.

"Hello Donald, I am calling you because we are on the way to East Orleans Hospital. Jacob has been shot."

Donald dropped the phone and Lynn kept trying to get him to respond. She finally hung up the phone realizing that he was probably on his way to the hospital.

As they pulled up, they saw Donald running into the emergency room.

He ran to the desk to inquire about his son. As Jackie and Lynn entered, they heard the receptionist give him Jacob's room number.

As they opened the door, Jackie felt like her legs were about to give out on her again. Seeing her child in that hospital bed was more than she could handle. She could not believe this day. Lisa was gone, and someone had tried to kill her son. How could she manage to tell Jacob about Lisa while he had been hurt himself? Somehow she would know when the time was right. She just knew it was not now. She just wanted to hug her child. She was so grateful that he was still breathing.

She went to give him a hug and squeezed him tightly. As she held onto her child, the tears began to flow. The thought of never being able to hug him again made her sick to her stomach.

"Mama, you can let go now."

Donald wanted to have some private time with his son. He was hopeful that Jacob would be willing to tell him everything. He knew that their relationship had been strained, but he wanted to put the past aside and just talk like a father and son should. He knew he had to wait, though. There was no way Jacob would give him the 411 with his mother right there. He would just have to wait for the right time. He was hoping to convince Jackie to let him spend the night; however, he knew that would be a tall order.

They all just sat there, not knowing quite what to say. Lynn announced she would be leaving in a few minutes.

"Jackie, if you want to, I can drive you back to the other hospital to pick up your car?"

Jacob was curious why his mother's car was at the hospital. He thought she probably went there to visit someone.

"No, I'll just leave it there, I know the parking fees will be horrendous, but, I just can't leave Jacob by himself."

"Jackie, I was going to ask you to let me spend the night with Jacob and you can come back in the morning."

Donald winked at her, hoping she could understand that this was a perfect time for him to resolve his issues with his child.

Lynn thought that was best as well.

"I think that is a great idea. You can come back early in the morning."

"Jacob, are you okay with that?"

"Go on, mama, I will see you tomorrow."

"I'll be back first thing in the morning," Jackie replied.

As Jackie and Lynn exited the room, Donald looked down at his child. He had a lot to say, he just did not know where to start.

Donald was happy to have this time alone with Jacob.

"Son, first I want to apologize for what has happened to us. I feel if I had been a better father, things would be different. My dad did not set a good example for me, and although I wanted to do better, I failed to give you what you needed."

"Yeah man, I have been angry with you for a long time," Jacob kept talking, while trying hard to hold back the tears.

"I don't even know when it all began. Man you were not there for me. I remember when I was little, how we would run around the house and play superman. It seems that when things got bad with you and mom, you forgot that I still needed you. We just lived in the same house. You never had time for me. We never connected. I wanted so badly for you to spend time with me. All you did was work and come home to the recliner and the TV. Man I hated you!"

"Son, I'm so sorry, please forgive me. Now I realize that I should have done more. I guess since I had no example of what being a father or a husband was, I just made a mess of things. You just cannot do what you never experienced. I don't want to give excuses for my behavior. I just did not realize that my baggage was affecting you and your mother."

"I think I was wrong too. I have been bitter because of you and mom. I could not believe that you could walk away like that. I think we both missed out on a lot."

"Yes we did. I wish I had been able to teach you how to navigate these streets and how to keep out of trouble. I was so caught up in my own pain, and had no idea the effect it would have on you. We will just need to begin again and put the past behind us. I really need you to tell me what you have been up to. We need to talk about who could have shot you, and why."

"I realize now that I have made some really bad choices. Since you were gone, I was determined to make my own way and not burden mom with caring for me. This guy named Jonathan asked me to do some dealing for him and he promised to fund my plan to start my own music production company. I have been making runs for Jonathan since I graduated."

"Son, didn't you know how dangerous this was?"

"Well, since I was just doing pickups and not handling the drugs, I thought I was okay."

"That is probably the worse part. You were carrying the money, man; everybody would have been after you."

"I never thought about it like that."

"Wait, I think Jonathan is the name of the guy that was shot in front of Lisa's house."

"What! Dad are you serious, when did this happen?"

"This evening about five-thirty." I heard it on the evening news."

"The gunman was clearly after Jonathan and the first bullet grazed him in his leg. When he fell down, Lisa stooped over to help him and a round of bullets hit her in the head. She died in her mother's arms on the front lawn."

"No! Please, God, no! Tell me it's not true; tell me it's not true. This is all my fault. Dad, this is my fault! I need to get to Lisa! I need to find out who did this! I swear, I will kill them! Whoever did this, they are a dead man. Trust me!"

Donald tried his best to console his son, but he could not get him to calm down. He wanted to leave the hospital. He tried to talk sense into his child to no avail. He called to the nurse's station and asked them to give Jacob a sedative. The nurse came in and Jacob was still insisting to leave the hospital. They gave him a shot and he cried himself to sleep. All he could think was his reason for living was over.

"Dad, this is my fault. I need to get to Lisa. I need to find out who did this. I swear, I will kill them! Whoever did this, they are a dead man! Trust me!"

He wished he had been killed instead of Lisa. This was all wrong.

She had not done anything to deserve this.

Jacob had a restless sleep, tossing and turning throughout the night.

When morning came, he was awakened by his mother's kiss on the cheek.

NaNa and Grandpa Joseph were with her and they both hugged him and asked him if he was okay.

"Mama, why didn't you tell me about Lisa? I still cannot believe this has happened. It's as if I am in a bad dream."

"I know son, it was so much going on, and that is why my car was at the hospital. I was in the kitchen and I did not hear the shots. I heard the doorbell ring and went to the door. When I opened the door, Jonathan was there, he told me Lisa had been shot. When I ran outside, she was already dead. I called 911 and followed the ambulance to the hospital."

"Mama, I cannot live with what I have done. This is all my fault. I was avoiding Lisa, so I called Jonathan and asked him to go by there to keep Lisa from looking for me. If I had not asked him to go by there, Lisa would still be alive."

NaNa and Grandpa Jacob looked at each other. The look on their faces was as if they had seen a ghost.

"Oh my God, Jacob," Jackie exclaimed. "This is horrible. The only way you are going to get through this is to ask for God's help. Do not try to play tough guy this time, son, it will not work."

Jackie had never seen Jacob like this before.

He kept saying, "I should be dead, I should be dead! Lisa didn't deserve this, man, it should have been me!"

She and Donald continued to request sedatives for their son.

When Labor Day came, Jacob was ready for discharge. His wounds were bandaged and he had been given a round of strong antibiotics. The doctors had ordered an evaluation to determine if Jacob was suicidal. He had managed to convince them that he was okay, but the truth was, he was far from okay. He just wanted to go home, talk to Jonathan and decide his next move.

The funeral was tomorrow morning. He did not know how he could possibly go. He did not have the courage to look Lisa's mom in the face.

CHAPTER FIFTEEN

THE FUNERAL

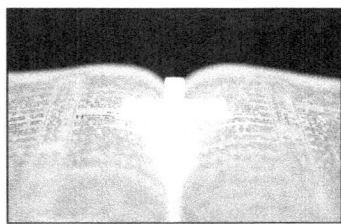

IT WAS THE MORNING OF THE FUNERAL. Jacob's mother made him take his anti-depressant medication before they left. His dad had spent the night in order to help his mother get him dressed. Jackie found it strange for him to be there, although comforting.

His dad dressed him, then picked him up and placed him in the wheelchair. Since both his legs were damaged, he could not put weight on either leg.

Jacob had dreaded this day since he first heard of Lisa's death. Part of him just wanted to stay home, but he knew Lisa would be there for him if the shoe were on the other foot. He just had to toughen up. His life would never be the same without her. He really had no desire to continue breathing.

They drove to the church in silence.

As his dad pulled into the parking lot, Jacob could feel his grief overtaking him. How could he go into the church and look at his sister in a casket?

As his dad picked him up and placed him in the wheelchair, he began talking to his son.

"We will get through this together, son. I know the pain is great, but it will get better with time."

"I don't know if I can go in there. It feels like I cannot breathe."

"Donald, let's just sit outside with him for a while until he is ready to go in."

"Alright son, we will sit out here for a little while, but you have to go in. We cannot miss the entire service."

"Okay, just give me a little time."

NaNa and Grandpa Joseph drove up and Jacob immediately sighed realizing that his attempt to get his parents to leave was thwarted, temporarily. His Nana got out of the car and proceeded to hug him. His mother began telling them that he was having trouble going in.

Grandpa Joseph attempted to reassure him.

"Son, God is not going to require anything of you that you do not have the ability to do. I know this is difficult, but ask the Holy Spirit to be with you and He will help you."

Jacob began to cry. They just did not understand. He did not see himself as being worthy of asking God anything, especially after what he had done to Lisa.

All of a sudden his mother pulled out this little red truck from her purse. She had been holding onto it since the night Lisa died. It seemed to bring her comfort.

"Son, do you remember this Christmas gift from Lisa right after they moved into the neighborhood?"

"Yes." His voice was muffled. He could barely speak.

"You always liked this truck. You all spent hours outside playing with it." His mother gave it to him. "Hold onto it, son. It will help you keep your mind on happy memories while you go through the service."

"Thanks, mom."

His dad took the wheelchair off the lock position and proceeded to wheel him into the church.

The minister had just begun to speak. He titled his sermon, An Angel Before Us. The minister gave countless incidences where Lisa had done selfless things for people in the community. Jacob turned his head to the right and noticed that Jonathan was sitting across from him. Their eyes met and it was as if they could not manage to look at each other. Then it was as if the minister's eyes moved back and forth from him and Jonathan. Jacob took his truck and held onto it tightly. He closed his eyes.

He immediately remembered the day after Christmas when he and Lisa ran around and around that tree. The memory brought a brief smile upon his face. He kept his mind on the memories and shut out the rest of the service. When it was time to view the body, his dad asked him if he wanted to go up. He shook his head and his dad left him alone.

When they got to the gravesite, Jonathan walked up to him.

"What's up, doc?

"Not much man, just trying to make it through this."

"Me too, dawg." What about me coming over to check on you?

"That would be fine."

His dad picked him up, placed him on the back seat, and they drove off.

When they got home, his mom and dad talked and they decided that he would go back to his apartment. She had told no one, but it was her plan to spend the night in the prayer room. She knew her son's future depended on it. Donald gave Jacob a sponge bath and put him to bed. He told Jackie good night.

"Donald, thank you for everything. I could not have made it through these few days without you."

"I needed to be there, not just for you and Jacob, but for me, too. I don't know what God has in store for us, but I would be willing to go back to counseling. Hopefully, we can get to a good place and be restored. I want that."

"Me too, Donald." He hugged his wife and walked to his car.

When Donald got to his apartment, the place seemed different. He had not realized how lonely his life was. He really wanted to talk to Jackie and explain how he felt, he was just afraid to do so. He did not know if she was ready to hear him. He knew he had to take a chance and call her. He prayed that she was open to hear him.

"Hello Jackie, got a minute?"

"Sure Donald."

"Well if we have any chance of being in a better place, I feel it is time for me to be totally honest with you. I spent so many years being angry with you; I did not take time to see that I was part of the problem. I spent most of our marriage being selfish. When you got pregnant the first time, I only thought about how it impacted what I wanted. Then when

Jacob was born, although we were in a better place financially, I still thought about my needs only. I spent so much time being angry about the changes that had taken place; I failed to appreciate what God had given me: a loving wife, and a beautiful son. All my childhood, when I was dealing with not having my basic needs met, I thought about how things would be different when I had my own family. Yet, when God blessed me with what I always dreamed of, I did not appreciate it. I have failed you and Jacob by abdicating my primary responsibility to make sure that all your needs were met. Somehow, I thought that just providing a roof over your head was sufficient, when your emotional needs were not considered at all. Can you find it in your heart to forgive me?"

Jackie replied, "Donald, I forgave you a long time ago. I am partly to blame too. I can't say that we were not supposed to be together, but I do think that I went ahead of God and married before we both were ready. I was just so determined to hurry and marry just to keep from fornicating. I was afraid that if I waited, I would not stay celibate until our wedding day. In order for us to have a healthy marriage, we should have gone through counseling to come into agreement about our differences in values. Now I feel that we have to go back and do it right this time. I think we should stay in counseling until God has brought us to a place of being in one accord. I got so frustrated, I stop praying for us. I just started praying for Jacob, knowing that God had made promises to me about him."

"Wait Jackie," Donald replied, "Don't be remorseful about the prayers you prayed for us. I do think God intervened and kept me when I was too vulnerable to keep myself. All those nights when I was not coming home, I bet you thought I was having an affair. I was so busy drowning my sorrows in alcohol; I had many nights where I was unable to drive home. My friend Roland would take me to his place and I would crash on his sofa."

"All those Fridays when I went to the club, I had began to do like the other guys. There was this one girl who always found me and we would dance the night away. I did tell her I was married, so things did not go any further. However, the weekend after I left home, I went to the club already wasted. I started telling her that we had separated and that I had an apartment at Lake Pontchartrain Apartments. I did not realize that she followed me home. When I answered the doorbell, there she was with a bottle of wine and two wine glasses. She said she came to celebrate my new home with me. I let her in, which was a big mistake. Next thing I knew, she was kissing me all over and I was responding to her affection. She started unbuttoning my shirt and I let her. Then, somehow I got the courage to ask her to leave. Jackie, I am convinced that the prayers you prayed kept me from violating my marriage. I just felt like I needed to tell you everything. I want things to be different. I don't want old baggage to stand in the way of what God is doing with us now."

"Donald, thank you so much for confiding in me. It does make me feel better that God was with us all the time. I know that God has done a good work in both our hearts and He is the one that is going to work in us until we are fully restored."

"Honey, I did not want to go to counseling with your pastor before, because I did not want to change. I know now that I must submit to counseling in the church, so we can see this miracle that God has started to full completion. Hope you rest well tonight, and please know that I love you with all my heart."

Jackie replied, "I love you too, Donald. Have a good night."

CHAPTER SIXTEEN

The Power of Reconciliation

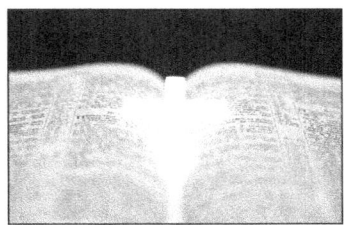

Jacob woke up and realized that he had slept with the truck in his hand. He had learned how to maneuver in his wheelchair, so he did not wait for his mother to help him get dressed. This was a Saturday. Normally, his day would be filled with runs to pick up the money. Now he had nothing to do. What he used to do no longer had any meaning. He looked over his life trying to figure out if he had done anything that was significant.

He now regretted his decision to stop going to church. Maybe if he was in a different place, Lisa might still be alive. He realized how empty his existence was. If only he saw some hope for a better future, maybe he would feel better. He knew he needed God now. He just did not know how to reach Him.

He pushed his chair outside to try and feel the morning breeze.

Jonathan walked up and they looked at each other. The agony that they were feeling could not be described in words.

Jacob started, "Man, my life is over. There is nothing left to live for."

Then Jonathan responded, "Man, I feel the same way. I know my life has been rough and I used that as an excuse to run these streets. I felt like, if I hurt, then somebody else needed to hurt too."

"Man, I hear you, and I know you had a rough life, but what is my excuse? My parents were good to me. They tried to give me the best life had to offer and I still made bad choices. The bottom line, no excuse is going to make us feel good about where we are. We just have to make our mind up to change."

They both turned around and saw the minister from Lisa's church pull up.

"Hello boys, you two have been on my mind since the funeral. I decided to try to look for you. You mind if we sit down under this tree?

Jacob spoke quickly, "I don't know, man, it seems a little eerie to me since this is the exact spot where Lisa was shot?

"I didn't know that, but this makes it the perfect spot for our conversation. This place of tragedy can be remembered as a place of miracles."

Jonathan proceeded to sit, but he was obviously uncomfortable too.

"I had a dream about you last night. God showed me how you have wrestled with Him. Your lives have been different, but God knows you better than you know yourselves. He knows how you were made and what you were created for. He also showed me how losing Lisa has affected you. I can see the hurt in your eyes and I sense that both of you no longer have a desire to live. You cherished her and are both angry with God because she is dead. You both blame God and wish you had been killed instead of her. I want you to know that although God knew that her life would be taken from her at an early age; it is not God Who is to blame. You see, God is a God Who will not violate the will of man.

"Let me explain. The man that shot Lisa had murder on his mind. God is so longing for man to freely love Him that he would not interfere with man's desire to make other choices. For this same reason, although He has longed for you to love Him, He has accepted your choice to sell drugs and reject him."

Jonathan looked up at the minister. "I don't understand."

"Jonathan, you were created to have a love relationship with God. God created you in His image. He created you with a physical body. He created you with a soul, which includes your mind, your will, and your emotions. The greatest part in you is your *spirit*. This is the part of you that is designed to be connected with God. The struggle that we must all overcome is that we must consciously *choose* to respond to our *spirit*, rather than our soul or will. God never intended for our soul to rule us. This is one of the things we struggle with as a result of the sin in the Garden of Eden."

"Wow! Jonathan replied. So you are telling me that there is a spirit inside of me that longs for God?"

"Yes, your spirit longs for God and God longs for you. He is just waiting for you to tell Him that you want Him too. I tell you guys, you will never regret giving your heart to God. It will change your world and you will have a freedom that you have never known."

Jacob replied, "You know what pastor? That is why Lisa always had a calmness that I never understood. Man, you mean we have been fretting all this time when God wanted us to just get connected with Him?"

"Yes, God has been waiting for you to choose Him. Lisa had been praying for both of you. She had talked to me many times about how much you were fighting surrendering to God's will. You know what? When that guy took Lisa's life, it was not the end for her. She just stepped into eternity.

"You see, only God can go back in time and walk into your places of sin and failure, then wipe that entire slate clean, as if it never happened. He wants to give you a hope and a new beginning. Let me ask you this: what if the situation had been different the other day and your life was taken? Where would you be right now?"

Jacob replied, "We would be in Hell!"

"Why don't you make the devil mad today? Give God your hand. Let this painful place be the place where you tell the devil no and tell God yes."

"Are you willing to do that?"

"Yes pastor, we both are."

The pastor lead both boys to the Lord, right under the tree that had been a place of many wonderful conversations, then a place of great tragedy.

Jonathan began running around the tree. "Man I feel so good now. It felt like I had the whole world on my shoulder. I am done with that old life. I feel at peace. Thank you God! You never gave up on me."

Lisa's mother heard all the commotion outside and she peeped out her window. After she saw her pastor, she opened the door.

Jacob was the first to announce. "Ms. Gloria, Jonathan and I just surrendered our life to God. We are so sorry for the pain that you are going through. Lisa is dead because of us. That is so unfair. The one person who had our back is gone and we are still here. Ms. Gloria, I promise you, I will dedicate the rest of my life to doing good things in honor of my best friend."

"Jacob, that does bring me some comfort because I know that Lisa would rejoice seeing you two doing God's will. I know the days ahead will be rough for me. It was easier to let Ronald go, seeing him in all that pain. The house is so empty now, but I know that God will not put more on me than I can bear."

Jacob replied, "Ms. Gloria. I will make it my responsibility to take care of you. I know I can't replace Lisa, but I can try to make you comfortable."

"I will help you too, Ms. Gloria."

The minister responded, "That's wonderful, guys, but God has many things in store for you. Please come by my office when you can. I want you all to speak to the youth at my church."

The minister left and Jonathan walked off after pushing Jacob's wheelchair inside his house.

Jonathan turned the corner to the next street. One of the guys from the opposing gang jumped out his car and starting pistol whipping him.

"Man, you thought that little bullet that hit your leg was bad, I'm about to smash you. I'm not going to make a mistake and shoot somebody innocent this time. You think you can outsmart me? You have met your match this time, man. When I finish with you I will leave your body stinking."

Jonathan was on the ground and the guy was stumping him and beating him in the head with the barrel of the gun.

"Man, when I finish with you, no one will recognize who you are. There won't be anything left to bury."

Jonathan started screaming. "You cannot take my life, man. I have already given it up."

"What are you talking about? You are crazy, man."

"You are right; I am crazy in love with Jesus. He has changed me, man."

The guy stopped hitting him in the head and stood him up.

"Listen man, I was all messed up. Lisa tried to show me a better way and I would not listen to her. If I had listened, she would still be alive. I promised her mom and I promised God that my life would be different. The pain of losing Lisa has made life hard to live, so if you kill me now, it would be okay with me. One thing I do know, I have peace now and I won't ever sell or use drugs again."

The guy pushed Jonathan to the ground.

"Man, you make me sick, Get away from me!"

"You might decide to kill me, but I have to tell you the truth. We were not created for this life we have chosen. We were created to have a strong connection with God. Unless you get connected with Him, you will have a life full of emptiness."

"Go away man, I want no part of you or your God."

"I used to feel the same way. Then the minister at Lisa's church explained to me that we are all created like God with a *spirit* designed to be connected to God. What happened was that things got messed up in the Garden of Eden, now we struggle because our soul dominates us and we have a will that chooses other things over God. Man, I am telling you, if you get connected, you won't regret it. It is so peaceful. Please, can I pray for you? Please?"

114

The guy shakes his head and Jonathan begins to pray.

"God, I have never prayed a day in my life, ah, ah. God I feel so connected to You now and I want Bro' man to feel it too. Touch him Lord; let the Spirit in him take over so he can feel connected to You too. And Lord, help us to change these streets for you, Amen."

"Jonathan, I am so sorry I killed that girl. She did not deserve that, man. I was blaming you and Jay for what I did, cuz you too tried to disrespect me. Man, I hope Ms. Gloria can forgive me and I hope God can forgive me, too. Tomorrow I will have to go and turn myself into the police."

"Man, you see that prayer you just prayed, God heard it and He just forgave you."

"Jonathan, I do feel better."

"I know man; this is the best feeling in the world." They embraced and walked away.

After Jonathan and the minister left, Jacob went inside and prepared for bed. He was so relaxed, he dosed off quickly. He heard soft music, and then he saw a bright light. Next thing he heard was Lisa's voice. He knew he was dreaming, but it was too good to be true. He told her how much he missed her and that he did not see how he could make it without her. He said he was sorry and he wished he would have listened to her and not been so stubborn. He also told her about his encounter with her pastor and that he had given up the street life and had accepted Jesus. Lisa told him all about heaven and how she was with her father, now. She wanted him to make sure that he forgave himself and lived to the fullest. It was so comforting for him to hear her voice. He slept like a baby that night.

The next morning, he got up and pushed his wheelchair to the kitchen to get some cereal. He was surprised that his mother was already up, since it was a Saturday.

Jacob was so happy to tell her about his dream. He told her that he knew God wanted him to forgive himself and go on with his life. He told his mother that he was going to start volunteering at the local community center to mentor young boys and try to discourage them from joining the gangs. He told her he knew that the streets could be dangerous, but he was ready to trust God to keep him.

Jackie was so happy to hear Jacob speak of God. She then began to tell him how she and his father had talked for a long time last night. She told Jacob that they were going to begin counseling with the pastor. She was so thankful that God had made everything work out for their good.

Jacob hugged his mother. He now understood how God worked and made miracles happen when we had no idea what was going on. He thought to himself, this Christian lifestyle is amazing.

SCRIPTURES TO PRAY OVER YOUR CHILDREN

Proverbs 18:21 says: "The tongue has the power of life and death."

As parents, we have the power to speak life or death to our children and over our children.

When we choose to speak the Word of God over our children, we are choosing to speak life over their lives.

Stand on the promises of Isaiah 55:11. These words will not return to you empty, but will accomplish and achieve the purpose for which they are sent.

Prayers before they are born:

"Lord, every good and perfect gift is from you. Please let this gift be born perfect, and without defects." (Psalm 127:3; James 1:17)

"Thank God that He is forming their inward parts in the depths of your womb and He has His hand on every part." (Psalm 139)

Prayers for their walk with God:

"That _____ will fulfill God's will and purpose for their life." (Psalm 138:8)

"Lord, teach _____ to perseverance in all they do, and help them especially to 'run with perseverance the race marked out for them.'" (Hebrews 12:1)

"That _____ will not be conformed to this world's system, but that they are constantly being transformed by the renewing of their mind, that they might know what is the good, acceptable, and perfect will of God for their lives." (Romans 12:2)

"I pray that _____ may grow in the grace and knowledge of our Lord and Savior Jesus Christ." (2 Peter 3:18)

"Father, help my children grow to find Your Word more precious than pure gold; and sweeter than honey, from the honeycomb. "(Psalm 19:10)

"Lord, hide your word in their hearts so that they don't want to sin against You." (Ps. 119:11).

"I pray that _____ may learn to live a life of love through the Spirit who dwells in them." (Ephesians 5:2, Galatians 5:22)

"Lord, please give _____ a strong craving for You, and a heart that clings passionately to You." (Psalm 63:8)

"Grant, Lord, that my children's lives may be marked by prayerfulness, that they may learn to pray in the Spirit on all occasions with all kinds of prayers and requests." (Ephesians 6:18)

"I pray that _____'s concept of themselves be solely defined by you, their creator, and that it is rooted in the realization that they are 'Your' workmanship, created in Christ Jesus." (Ephesians 2:10)

"That _____ shall love the Lord their God with all their heart and with all their soul and with all their mind." (Matthew 22:37-39)

Prayers for their relationship with their parents:

"I thank You Father, that _____ will honor and obey me, therefore, _____ will please the Lord and will live a long life." (Exodus 20:12; Ephesians 6:2.)

"That _____will learn to obey us and that we will not do anything to embitter or discourage him." Col 3:20-21

Prayers for their relationships with others:

"May _____be an example to others in life, in love, in faith, and in purity." (I Timothy 4:12)

"God, help _____ to 'act justly,' 'love mercy,' and 'walk humbly' in all they do." (Psalm 11:7, Micah 6:8)

"Father, grant _____ the ability to 'show proper respect to everyone,' as Your Word commands." (1 Peter 2:17)

"Let love and faithfulness never leave _____, but bind these twin virtues around their necks and write them on the tablet of their hearts." (Proverbs 3:3)

"Lord, please cultivate in _____ the ability to show true humility toward all." (Titus 3:2)

"Lord, please clothe _____ with the virtue of compassion." (Colossians 3:12)

"That _____ would flee the evil desires of youth, and pursue righteousness, faith, love and peace, along with those who call on the Lord out of a pure heart." (2 Timothy 2:22)

Prayers for God's Blessings:

"That _____ will be blessed and will be mighty in the land." (Psalm 112:2)

"That _____would be without blemish, well-favored in appearance and skillful in all wisdom, discernment, and understanding, apt in learning knowledge, competent to stand and serve in the king's palace—and to teach others." (Daniel 1:4)

Prayers for Purity:

"That _____ will flee from all sexual immorality and impurity in thought, word or deed, and they will realize that their body is the temple of the Holy Spirit." (I Corinthians 6:18-19)

"Create in _____ a pure heart, O God, and let their purity of heart be shown in their actions." (Psalm 51:10)

Prayers for Salvation:

"Lord, let salvation spring up within _____, that they may obtain the salvation that is in Christ Jesus, with eternal glory." (Isaiah 45:8; II Timothy 2:10)

"God, please give _____ a new heart and put a new spirit within them; please take the heart of stone from them and give them a heart of flesh. Please put Your Spirit within them and cause them to walk in Your statutes, and they will keep Your judgments and do them." (Ezekiel 36:26-29)

BOOK CLUB DISCUSSIONS FOR PARENTS

—Jacob wrestled until he recognized it was God.

   a. Are there areas in your life or your children's lives where you are wrestling with God? Can you identify them?

   b. Can you figure out what is holding you back from total surrender? Jackie was aware that prayer was her greatest weapon, do you feel that your prayer life is adequate? If not, why?

—Donald and Jackie were raised differently. Oftentimes, he did not understand why she was so adamant about her prayer life and her faith. Do you think she was judgmental? Why or why not?

Do you think her decision to marry Donald was bad timing or a bad decision? Why?

What about the night club scene? Was she inconsiderate when she did not want to go after Jacob was born? Do you think she was fair? What do you think about her compromise?

What about her and Donald's relationship? Are there other things both of them could have done to keep them from growing apart?

How about her relationship with her son? Do you think there were other things she could have done to reach out to him? Please expound.

What about her relationship with her mother? Do you think she was too dependent on needing her opinion for everything?

Jonathan and Jacob had wounds that affected them and led them to engage in self-destructive behavior, and although they were unaware that these wounds were affecting them, their life choices were influenced by this baggage. Can you identify the wounds that caused them to be self destructive?

We are all victims of our life experiences. Can you identify your wounds and determine how they have affected the decisions you have made?

Oftentimes, women are left with the sole responsibility for the children. As with Jackie, although there may be a male in the home, he may not take as much of an active role in the rearing of the children, which leaves a void for the children, both male and female. Please discuss ways to resolve or reduce the affects of missing a strong relationship with a male father figure.

BOOK CLUB DISCUSSIONS FOR YOUTH

1. Jacob wrestled until he recognized it was God.

   a. Are there areas in your life where you are wrestling with God? Can you identify them?

   b. Can you figure out what is holding you back from total surrender?

2. Jacob struggled with both his parents. Can you identify with what he was feeling? Please expound.

3. Can you identify areas where you struggle relating to your parents? As a group, can you identify ways that may rectify the problem?

4. Jonathan and Jacob had wounds that affected them and led them to engage in self-destructive behavior, and although they were unaware that these wounds were affecting them, their life choices were influenced by this baggage. Can you identify the wounds that caused them to be self destructive?

5. We are all victims of our life experiences. Can you identify your wounds and determine how they have affected the decisions you have made?

www.ingramcontent.com/pod-product-compliance
Lightning Source LLC
Chambersburg PA
CBHW051256170626
46809CB00004B/1670